Lonesome Standard Time

Lonesome Standard Time

DANA ANDREW JENNINGS

Harcourt Brace & Company

NEW YORK SAN DIEGO LONDON

Requests for permission to make copies
of any part of the work should be mailed to:
Permissions Department, Harcourt Brace & Company,
6277 Sea Harbor Drive, Orlando, Florida 32887-6777.

Library of Congress Cataloging-in-Publication Data
Jennings, Dana Andrew.
Lonesome standard time: a novel/Dana Andrew Jennings.—1st
ed.
p. cm.
ISBN 0-15-200778-4
I. Title.
PS3560.E5175L66   1996
813'.54—dc20   95-6477

Printed in the United States of America
First edition
A B C D E

FOR MY SECOND PARENTS,

MIRIAM AND EVAN KRIEGER,

WITHOUT HESITATION

Hunt's Station, L.S.T.

Hunt's Station vanished from maps years ago, and faded from memory before that, even. Isn't captured on any road signs either, except for those so weary and so weather-whipped you can't read them . . . or trust them. The towns next door barely remember their neighbor. To them Hunt's Station isn't a town at all but a rumor of a town—like an older step-brother you've heard stories about but never met. To get to Hunt's Station, you either have to be born to it or unlucky. The town squats off a logging trail off a washboard, which is off an exit of an exit to a two-lane road that sees maybe twenty cars a day . . . fewer on weekends. One way in, one way out. Hunt's Station is a place where the rumble of heavy trucks lulls the men to sleep most nights and keeps the women awake . . . where black heartwounds fester and dark springs mutter in the deep woods . . . where soot-peppered goblin snow, misshapen and rock-hard, prevails till June . . . where old-time fiddlers coax timber rattlers into their fiddles and banjo pickers blister the strings till their fingers bleed . . . where the air is always tarnished by smoke from Fire Town . . . where men limp and are missing fingers . . . where ghost rails coil into town and just stop . . . where you swear the raincrows can talk and sometimes, even, run the town. No babies have been born in Hunt's Station for nearly twenty years; and all the dogs and cats are so old they don't chase each other anymore. When the schoolhouse burned a few years back, the town didn't rebuild. No one complained. And the churches—once there were a half-dozen in town— have either burned or been spurned and abandoned. In Hunt's Station, the women's faces burn with fierce beauty carved by decades of betrayal and sadness; touch one of those sharp, saint faces, take away a bleeding hand. Those women . . . they put on their old gray dresses to waltz together in the pouring rain. They always stop to listen to the whine of a distant train, no matter what they're doing. They smile and nod at crow gossip, but shudder at the remembered moan of a full-moon owl. Not a one of them cries anymore—those rivers dried long ago— but most of them play fiddle . . . sobbing fiddle . . . fiddle that wails with the cries of too many babies left unborn. You can see it as they play, fiddle cradled between chin and shoulder. The skin tightens over keen cheekbones and smolders fever red as the fiddle bow dips and the fiddle bow saws. And when they close their eyes, those deep wells of sadness, they cross over the line . . . and they're on Lonesome Standard Time.

Part One

1

Infamous Angel

High, lonesome, her voice breaks over the town like bleak November rain.

Some nights it's a kind of revelation, an angel choir bound in one voice. On others, it's plain North Country granite sanded to tears. She sings as if each breath were her last, so desperate, somehow trying to carry her people to higher ground single-handed. Her voice, which carries the way a train whistle will past midnight, is a voice for the end of things, a voice that most nights haunts Hunt's Station in its darkest hour.

Keegan lives for that voice.

Keegan is a stranger, a journalist, doing time in a dying (some say already dead) town. And Clare Hunt's singing is one of the few things that brings him any measure of joy. Keegan believes he is stalking the story of his life . . . and it's killing him.

She sings gospel songs and town songs—pain songs flensed from the heart—and sometimes she's a pure spirit voice hymning in the tongues of brook and stream, wind in the trees, and riven granite, weeping her weary blues and letting them writhe where they may.

In a town too withered for tears, it has fallen upon Clare Hunt to leach each day's poisons.

The singing stopped sudden as it started, bringing a silence more profound than before, like right after a train rumbles by, or after making love. A silence where the air is supercharged and has thickened so it seems you could suffocate. A silence, ultimately, of disappointment.

Keegan sighed and capped his pen, a plain old clear nineteen-cent Bic—though he doubted they cost nineteen cents anymore . . . except in Hunt's Station. He hadn't written by hand since grammar school—he'd even raised his shiny schoolboy's writing callus—but his personal computer wouldn't work in Hunt's Station. Neither would his fax machine, cellular phone, or VCR, and his color TV crackled black-and-white with the two stations that managed to sneak into the valley. He didn't mind writing longhand though. It slowed him, made him think harder, see more clearly. He liked hunching over the page like some nineteenth-century bookkeeper, his left hand resting light on his right shoulder and chin propped on his left forearm . . . liked hearing the scritch-scratch of pen on sweat-damp paper as his lips worked soundlessly . . . liked how the words wobbled and swayed, shrank and grew according to his mood. No, the writing wasn't Keegan's problem. Never had been. Writing had always been Keegan's solution, and even when it hadn't been, he'd been able to pretend.

He grabbed a couple beers, homebrew in scummy brown

bottles, walked downstairs, and gave in to the front steps; his book could wait. The beer bottles sweated in the muggy night. But even in that heavy, hiding-under-the-bed air, he could smell Fire Town.

The beer was thick, almost loamy, and bitter. But Keegan liked the taste. Had even, within the first minute of ever tasting it, transmuted it from mere beer to metaphor; to Paul Keegan, this beer, brewed by one Dirty Willy Menard, *was* Hunt's Station, and he wouldn't've traded a single bottle for a case of the skunk piss that passed for beer outside town. Rolling that beer on his tongue, letting it pickle his taste buds, Keegan imagined he could taste the tears and sweat upon which Hunt's Station had been built, the smoke and ash as constant as the rounds made by the trucks from Hunt Waste Management and, yes, the toxins, the town's self-inflicted cancer, the rotted core that had drawn him and his talent for decay to this town north of nowhere.

Keegan snorted, laughing at himself, and said, "Keegan, you dub. A beer's a beer." He cracked the second.

He stared at the old Hunt Place perched atop Main Street, as if he could somehow conjure Clare Hunt. He had never seen her—no one saw her anymore, unless they dared the walk up her red brick steps. But Clare's voice stirred in him the same feelings that Reverend Shook's sermons had when he was a boy. A feeling that furry, holy rodents were scurrying in his stomach. His quivery insides wouldn't quiet till the next Sunday morning, and then the reverend would just go and rile him up all over again. It'd almost been a relief when the church elders had forced Reverend Shook out. Keegan had always wondered what'd happened to the reverend. What was the story line?

His religion now, if he had to confess one, was narrative journalism, that subjective alchemy of fact, quote, impression, and intuition that, when it worked, created an entire world on the black-and-white flatland of the printed page, gave dimension to people and place, and, one hoped, left the reader changed—if just a little. A long way from the Laconia (N.H.) *Evening Citizen* and schoolboy basketball. His gods were the writers who, more often than not, made the reader believe that they had indeed swallowed the burning sword whole: A. J. Liebling and Tom Wolfe, John McPhee and Joseph Mitchell.

The beer, as it should, stung especially bitter at bottle's bottom. Keegan balanced the empty on his palm and looked back up the stairs, debating whether to wallow or slog back up for a refill or two. Luxuriating in his indecision, he slithered down the stairs, propped his head on the bottom step, and nested his heels in the gravel of Main Street. He smiled, shut his eyes. At two beers past midnight, Hunt's Station seemed almost livable.

He heard the truck long before he saw it, creaking and groaning through the night woods toward Main Street, heard the thud of the ripe, fifty-five-gallon steel drums. More work for Hunt Waste Management, more poison to be swallowed by Hunt's Station, another footnote. Keegan wondered what Hunt's Station had been like on that first day when one of those black trucks slunk out the woods. Before Sanborn Hunt had betrayed his town and its people, and before those people had shut their eyes, opened their hands, and waited for the bite of sharp, new twenty-dollar bills.

Sanborn Hunt had surely brought money into Hunt's Station—and no one who wanted a job ever went begging, not even Keegan—but he never brought prosperity.

The truck nosed out the woods and lurched down Main

Street, steel drums muttering. Keegan blinked at the headlights as the truck grunted to a stop in front of him.

"Beer?"

"That you, Willy?"

"Yut."

"Where you coming in from?"

"Some shit-hole . . . Upstate New York. Beer?"

"Yeah, okay."

Dirty Willy handed down the rimed bottle. Willy Menard never went nowhere without his ice chest.

"That one hurts good, Willy."

"Lots more."

"Need help unloading this mother?"

"Always."

"Well?"

"Climb on in."

Dirty Willy, brewmaster and wastehauler, jammed the truck into gear and rolled down Main Street toward Hunt Waste Management.

" 'Nother beer?"

The cab of Dirty Willy's truck, like Willy himself, reeked of grease, gasoline, and beer. Keegan wondered whether the guy was ever sober, or whether he maybe had moved beyond drunk and sober to where beer was the same to him as food and water was to other people. The floor brimmed with a workingman's mulch of oil rags, beer bottles, matches, dismembered road maps, fast-food wrappers, chicken feathers and wayward wrenches and screwdrivers; Keegan had to excavate with his feet to find the floor. A cardboard air freshener the shape of a pine tree dangled from the radio.

Dirty Willy drove with both stubby hands on the wheel and a sweating beer in his crotch as the truck snaked deeper into the woods toward Hunt Waste Management. The steel drums griped in the back—workers told they have to put in overtime.

"Don't know what's better on a smotherin' night like this," Dirty Willy said, "drinking this here beer or just letting it set right there between my legs."

Then he laughed, a wicked, lip-curdling snort that detonated a cough so harsh that Dirty Willy had to stop the truck. Willy spasmed as the cough tore through him, his hands strangling the steering wheel, feet stamping the floor, forehead yanked forward as if by the hair. The cords rippled on his neck. Keegan waited, quiet, the way you wait out a sudden summer thunderstorm. The Hunt's Station cough didn't spook him anymore. He'd even written a chapter about the cough in his book.

Finally, Dirty Willy cleared his throat, hawked out the window, demolished his beer in a gulp, and flipped the empty into the night.

"Christ!" he said, his breath idling down. "Feels like I hacked up half a lung."

By way of conversation, Keegan popped the ice chest, handed Willy another beer, and took a long pull on his own.

They unloaded in silence, Keegan working the truck bed, Dirty Willy the mouth. Keegan had put on his rubber gloves and steel-toed boots; but Dirty Willy worked barehand and in black, high-top sneakers; some people wondered whether Dirty Willy didn't bathe in the poison that arrived at Hunt Waste Management. The fifty-five-gallon steel drums were stacked two-high, and Keegan tugged one down, its semi-solid contents slightly sloshing, let it thud to the floor, then shoved it to Dirty Willy, who grabbed it and dropped it to the ground. Keegan liked the rhythm of unloading a truck, liked how his muscles and those of the guys he worked with fell into line and pistoned together to whittle away at the job. It was hard—sometimes dangerous—but it was basic Point A to Point B, bone-grinding labor. Work. A job. And the longer Keegan worked at Hunt Waste Management he sometimes forgot he was working there as a reporter. Forgot that by unloading the trucks and stacking the drums that he was helping put the finishing touches to his subject.

Done, Keegan and Willy slumped against the truck's bumper and killed beers, more WillyBrew. Keegan didn't understand why he was still in Hunt's Station. He'd gathered what he needed for his book. He should go. He had no more questions. Needed no more answers. He had just the right amount of information to write. If he stayed too much longer, he might never finish the book.

Keegan spit. "I'm sick of this fucking place."

"Ain't no one asked you here."

"Goddamned sick."

"No one asking you to stay."

Dirty Willy stood. "Just you remember, Mister Man," he said. "You ain't at home—we are."

Keegan heeled away. Didn't even turn when Dirty Willy started the truck and grumbled off.

The earth, always swampy, even in high summer, sucked at Keegan's boots as he trudged across Hunt Waste Management to the hiss and trickle of hemorrhaging holding tanks, the steel moan of drums expanding and contracting, the generator hum. But no mosquitoes. It was a muggy midsummer's night and there were no mosquitoes; Keegan realized he'd never seen any insects at HWM. Another detail. Another sentence for the book, maybe two. He shook his head; it *was* time to leave.

The lagoon, a good fifty yards in diameter, oozed at the heart of Hunt Waste Management. It wasn't HWM's only lagoon—dozens lay hidden on Sanborn Hunt's hundreds of acres—but it was the biggest and the first, just a hole, really, draped with a liner that had never been as impermeable as Sanborn Hunt claimed . . . or pretended. A weeping black wound that would never heal, the poisoned abyss into which Hunt's Station had fallen. A place to be baptized by the devil. A dumping ground that Sanborn Hunt, for his wealth of weasel words, could never justify. Taking on more business than he could handle, Sanborn Hunt had simply dug a pit, called it a lagoon, and started to dump. Had let his town drown in the pus of the twentieth century.

Keegan sometimes wished that he had never stumbled upon this place, had never noticed the raven-black trucks crammed with fifty-five-gallon steel drums that skulked along the highways, had never decided to follow one home. Keegan hadn't needed to know that such a place as Hunt's Station existed. But once he did know, there was no flinching. The story was too good, the narrative pull too strong.

That goddamned lagoon had swallowed him too.

Out in the black woods, a banjo, picked one note at a time, pierced the night. Spare, deliberate, each note raw and sharp, trying to cut through something more than the dark, waiting for an answer.

Call . . . but no response. Not just blue notes . . . but black notes. Notes that could have leached from any one of those steel drums. A night picker, playing not just banjo but Keegan's heart too.

Keegan leaned against the chain-link fence that circled Sanborn Hunt's lagoon, cradled an imaginary banjo, plucked along with this night picker. He shut his eyes, crabbed his hands, and heard nothing but the notes shredding his heart.

The next morning, they found Paul Keegan floating face down in the lagoon.

"Christ on a crutch," said Joe Bleak, the foreman. "Someone run and get old Sanborn, quick."

2

Crossroads

Trolling up Route 316, spooling back home to Hunt's Station, Hank Rodgers saw that Miles' Grant hadn't changed much in fifteen years. As his Datsun 210 bumped along the unrepentant cement highway, Hank took in the Old Kerry Ginger Ale water tank—IF IT'S O.K., IT'S OLD KERRY—fresh-painted green and gold; Caillouette's General Store still snugged to the train tracks; Charlie's Barber Shop blazing silo-red, the red-white-and-blue barber pole still shattered from when Charlie punched it out after the Red Sox gave away Game Seven of the 1975 World Series to the Reds; and the Miles' Grant Drive-In Movie Theatre, its broad whitewashed screen like a giant bedsheet hung out to dry. And as he drove, Hank shivered, like being touched on the arm by a woman you think you could fall in love with.

Even so, Miles' Grant was just a town, mere prologue. Hunt's Station was the past. You could be found in Miles' Grant. In Hunt's Station, you could hide forever.

Some two miles past the drive-in, a dirt road snuck up on

Route 316—a road only a native would know—and stuck its nose out the summer-green woods. Hank yanked the Datsun hard right and began his descent toward Hunt's Station. But the road, which had been part of the route to town when he was a kid, had given in to those woods. Branches lashed and slashed at the car; that puckerbrush-choked road had once been wide enough for two pickups to pass, a mutt lolling serenely out each window.

The dirt road—maybe not even a road anymore, just a path that remembered being a road—opened out on a paved, two-lane highway that sawed straight through the woods. To Hank's right, the highway dead-ended at a hill of gravel in which he'd seen more than one car buried to the back door. Still wasn't Hunt's Station. But it was walking distance.

He swung the Datsun left and picked up speed on The Whispering Turnpike.

As straight and black and smooth as a father's leather belt, The Whispering Turnpike seemed to bend your ear and hiss, "Go faster . . . go faster, damn it!" A death road. A road that devoured teenaged boys who didn't know better . . . and restless men who were sick and tired of knowing better. All up and down The Whispering, white crosses clustered, marking each spot where the road had tasted blood; there were more than Hank cared to count.

As he kicked the Datsun past sixty, it seemed to Hank he was again being chased by those homegrown hellhounds that had made him flee New York City. And he pushed the car toward eighty, where it got the steel palsy and began to shudder. But Hank paid no mind.

He liked the prickle of the road wind trying to scalp him, liked watching the white lines flicker like lizard tongues. Liked the lightness. The faster he drove, the lighter he became, throwing down burdens, peeling back years: sixteen again, bombing home from the drive-in movies with Clare Hunt on a hot summer's night, both of them laughing, in love, their town already dying but them too young to realize, or care. Sixteen, and both of them sworn to escape Hunt's Station, neither able to imagine the future without the other. Sixteen, in a small town, and not knowing a good-goddamned thing.

Hank glanced down, clicked on the radio, didn't see the crow-black truck bolt from the side road; dozens of side roads darted at this highway . . . starved snakes.

The Datsun clipped the truck's rear end and flipped, a four-cylinder quarter, and rocked and rolled down The Whispering Turnpike. The car tumbled a good fifty yards before it jerked to a stop, quivering on all fours.

Hank shut the car, unhooked his seat belt. The air reeked of smoke, not the calming smoke of wood burning or tobacco, but a chemical smoke like burning paint, and he thought of his father; everything still, so quiet . . . Hank swore he could hear atoms humming. His arms, already swelling, were black and blue and bleeding. His head hurt, his right knee, his chest. He stared at the web of the shattered windshield . . . shook his head . . . still alive.

The door, wedged to the frame, wouldn't budge, so he crawled out the open window. The Datsun's roof had caved in—somehow not enough to crush him—and the left front had crumpled where he hit the truck; two tires were flat.

"Ain't it somethin', what a man can walk away from."

Hank turned.

"Hell of a way to come back home," said Dirty Willy. "Hell of a way, Hank Rodgers."

Willy . . . sonuvabitching Dirty Willy . . . Hank *was* almost home.

"Still driving like a fucking maniac, huh, Willy?" Hank said. This was, after all, Dirty Willy Menard, who never let a year pass without totaling at least one of Hunt Waste Management's trucks. It had almost become a point of pride with Willy, who shrugged and said, "I ain't the one hit a truck going eighty miles an hour."

"Got me there."

Hank stuck out his hand, Willy spit on his and rubbed it hard on his dungarees, then they shook.

"Long time, no see," Hank said.

"Want a beer?" Dirty Willy asked.

Dirty Willy gave Hank a ride down to The Crossroads. Not quite Hunt's Station, but the last place where a truck or a car could turn around before town.

"I'll call in to the shop and get someone to take care of your car," Willy shouted as he drove off. "Take it easy."

"Thanks, Willy."

Hank watched the truck till it stuttered out of sight, the empty fifty-five-gallon steel drums banging and clanging, an almost happy sound; those ringing tones were muted, darker when the drums came back to town full.

Hank Rodgers set his suitcase in the center of The Crossroads and sat on it facing due north . . . a straight shot to the heart of the past. He didn't know where the nameless east–west road led that helped make this crossroads; all he knew was that it had nothing to do with Hunt's Station . . . never had, never would.

His arms had stopped bleeding, he'd used one of Dirty

Willy's beers to wash the gashes, but his whole body ached, his head still throbbed. He yawned, stretched. It'd been a long trip. Not quite ready to go home, Hank pulled a pair of dungarees out of his suitcase, rolled them tight and, using them for a pillow, fell asleep beneath a shade tree.

Hank woke as dusk's last faint grays faded and night's ink pooled in the woods. He listened to the riffling prayers of the night leaves, watched the lightningbugs blink and bob, smelled sweet pitchy summer borne on dark breezes. He was tempted to spend the night there, stretched out at the old Crossroads, committed to neither the past nor to the future.

Waiting . . . hiding . . . like his old man.

He sighed. He hadn't come this far back just to shake hands with Willy Menard, drink a beer and turn around. He had some walking to do.

But as he tried to stand, Hank found that his body had seized up while he slept. It seemed every joint, every muscle had gone to rust, and he slumped back. He'd almost forgotten the accident till then.

"Christ," Hank said. "Christ."

Leaning on his sleeping tree, Hank oozed himself up this time, gave his aching bones some warning, picked up his suitcase and headed north, toward home.

As he walked the night woods, just another shadow among shadows, Hank realized he felt happier than he had in a long time, and that the closer he got to Hunt's Station, the happier he felt. Though he'd been desperate to escape Hunt's Station as a kid, he wondered whether the town had made him unfit to live anywhere else. Wherever he'd lived, wherever he'd worked, he'd never fit in . . . or, more important, felt he had never fit in. Ill at ease, he had always rocked on the balls of his feet, a skittish animal ready to run. He was master of the thousand-yard stare, the Hunt's Station stare, and it chilled people. And his marriage—how he'd managed to marry, he never knew—drowsed, suspended like week-old milk in that moment before it curdles. He and his wife had agreed to spend the summer apart; really, she had told him and he'd simply shrugged yes; he'd left his wedding band in the apartment, dangling from the key rack hung at the front door, more final than any divorce papers.

So, yes, the night woods suited him, suited Hank Rodgers very well.

A granite post, four foot tall, is all that marks passage into Hunt's Station proper; a town bent on vanishing doesn't brag on itself to strangers. The post is planted under an ancient oak, Raven's Roost, where sometimes it seems that every raven and crow in the woods gathers to gossip. Some people in Hunt's Station spend their days gabbing with these ravens and crows . . . and nobody else.

Hank stopped at the post . . . the past; he saw nothing in the tree's black guts, but knew he was watched. When he had sped past that post on his way out of town fifteen years before, he had thought that was the end. He hadn't understood then the claims that a place like Hunt's Station makes on its children, the raging scars it leaves, its constant haunting pull—no matter how many miles, no matter how many years distant. Hank kneeled at the post, the granite rough and warm, his hand roaming . . . knobby here, concave there . . . sharp, then smooth . . . raw, crooked granite ripped from the earth, sledged back in, and ornery as ever. That granite felt right to Hank, felt like home.

He grabbed his suitcase, took a deep breath, and stepped into Hunt's Station.

Right away, he smelled Fire Town—a lace of smoke embroidering the heavy air—and he smiled. He'd come of age at the edges of Fire Town, and the smell of that bitter, loamy smoke was redolent of home. He could never smell smoke, any kind of smoke, without thinking of his father. He walked on.

The first fiddle sounded deep in the woods, a mother calling a child a long ways home to supper. A second fiddle moaned nearer, mournful, the notes stretched . . . slow . . . thick as fresh-laid tar. Hank jumped at the third, which called to the others from close by and picked up the pace, a train hell-bent on hitting open country, as other fiddles rang in. The fiddle music, blood music to Hank, gusted through the night woods and shepherded him toward town: "Hunt's Hill Hobo" and "Old Crow Can't Jump" and "Fire Town Frolic," each song a page from his boyhood, each song written by his father.

The woods swelled with the music of the night fiddlers, and Hank couldn't imagine how many played out there—the same way you can't count a summer night's cricket chorus—tucked in the dark just as the fiddles were tucked under their chins, bowing their strings, sawing him home.

Eventually, one by one, the fiddles dropped away, but the air still pulsed with their passage, and Hank suddenly found himself out of the woods and about to step onto Main Street, the only road in Hunt's Station that had its own sign. But, still, that first lone fiddle sobbed in the deep woods, that mother still calling her child home, and then Hank shuddered, knew that one fiddle would always wail because that mother's child was never coming home.

The old Hunt place glowering at his back, Hank stood atop Main Street and looked down into town—empty, quiet, except for the warm glow from Marian's Cafe. He'd eaten his last meal in Hunt's Station at Marian's. His old man smoking filterless Luckies and swilling black coffee thicker than the poison in Sanborn Hunt's lagoons, Hank had put away six eggs fried over easy (Marian had a way with yolks), half a pound of bacon, a mountain of home fries, and more wheat toast (buttered on both sides) than he could remember; it was as if he thought he might never eat a square meal again. Sometimes, when things had gotten too rough between him and his old man, Hank had taken a room over Marian's; he smiled at the memory of waking mornings to the café murmur, the smell and sputter of a dozen breakfasts frying.

He started down the hill toward Marian's and felt as if he were wading into a familiar swimming hole . . . knew where, without warning, the water yawned from four foot to ten foot . . . as if fifteen years had never passed.

A man and woman stepped out of Marian's, the man holding the screen door for the woman, and Hank stopped. The man loosened his belt, the woman tugged at the bottom of her blouse. He pointed to something across the road and the woman nodded. The man lit a cigarette and the two of them walked down Main Street without touching. But after a few seconds, the woman looked up at the man as if considering him for the first time in her life, and her fingers lurched toward his until their hands laced.

Hank watched them drift down the street, two cinders about to blink out, until he couldn't see them anymore.

Hard wind blew from the West at daybreak. A cloud-eating, marrow-tingling wind that jacked the sky higher and painted it the dark blue of a newborn's eyes. A scouring wind that kept Fire Town's smoke at bay, a wind meant to dry clothesline-clinging clothes, that seemed to whittle away worry, straighten backs, and make Hunt's Station almost livable. Hunt's Stationers called it an Angel Wind, as if some rambling angel had stopped just outside town to beat her powerful wings and bless the undeserving with her holy breeze.

Hank shivered awake to the snap and flap of windblown white cotton curtains. The room smelled of dawn's dew-soaked grass. He kicked back his sheet, shut his eyes, let the wind break over him.

Marian, acting as if he had never been away, had put Hank up in his old room, had explained to him that some guy named Keegan's belongings were still in it. She hadn't had the patience to tell him that this Keegan was dead, had been fished out of Sanborn Hunt's lagoon. Why, after all, ruin a weary man's good sleep?

Hank still felt the car crash in his sore bones and muscles, but his cuts and gashes had crusted overnight and some bruises were already yellowing toward health.

"Somebody ought to hang that goddamned Dirty Willy," he muttered. But maybe, he thought, maybe the crash had been the price of coming back home, to shed his city skin.

He tugged on his dungarees, which were as morning stiff as he was, pulled on a clean white T-shirt—his father's uniform, he realized—and walked downstairs.

Wind eddying, sun lazing in the East (more felt than seen), Hank Rodgers walked down the middle of Main Street, the gravel night-damp, the town still sleeping . . . Fire Town—and his father—on his mind.

Roads had narrowed in fifteen years, woods taking back its own. Seemed to Hank that if he wasn't careful one of those trees might lurch out and mug him or one those bushes run a shoot and trip him. And even with the Angel Wind, once he got a couple miles from Main Street, there was no shaking the stink from Hunt's Station's constant burning wreck. Fire Town . . . Devil Town.

Most the houses out that way, toward his father's, had been abandoned: the Perkins place, the Haywards', the Van Dorens'. Skeletons scabbing back roads whose names had been forgotten . . . former footholds on the land back on their heels, cringing . . . rooves concave . . . bitter smoke roaming barren rooms . . . loose, grayed boards losing form and meaning . . . dense, biting fences of branch and briar . . . a tire swing swaying riderless in the wind. Ghost houses and their architecture of despair: crumbled chimneys, shattered windows, front doors gaping, shingles flapping.

Though he smelled the thickening smoke, felt it smart his eyes and coat his throat, Hank was disappointed somehow that these families had given in, not to Fire Town itself but to the mere threat of Fire Town. He didn't blame them for leaving, really. But the Hunt's Stationers he'd grown up among had always liked a good fight—even, maybe especially, one they couldn't win.

Hank's father had liked to say, " 'Bout the only way you

can make a Hunt's Stationer stay beat is by killing him, and I ain't even a hundred percent on that."

Smoke bound the woods. A caustic coil twisting, twining through the trees, writhing at Hank's passing. When Hank'd been a kid the thick smoke, the killing smoke, had never snaked this far toward town. He realized that his father didn't live on the edge of Fire Town anymore, that he no longer hunched on the backsteps after supper, savoring his dessert cigarette, and watched Fire Town's gray ghosts, some hundred yards distant, waltz toward evening. His father *lived* in Fire Town now; his old man had become one of the ghosts.

Hunt's Stationers call Fire Town "hell's upper story": the place where smoke billows from charred earth, where snow melts on the black steaming ground and rain sizzles, where water runs scalding from cold-water faucets. No one knows what kindled the inferno that feeds beneath Fire Town—well, no one admits to knowing, anyway. All Hunt's Stationers will say is that the burning started some years after Sanborn Hunt brought his damned factory to town—no one's quite sure how many—and that the poison fumes seeping from the earth there sure reek a lot like Hunt's Waste Management. Each year the fire slowly, but surely, grows, like a nailhead spreading with age.

Hank crested Mama's Hill; that's what he and his sisters, Alison and Iris, had called it. When they'd been little, the top of that hill was as far as they were allowed to go from the house alone. Sometimes, there wasn't anything more fun in the world than to sit at the very tiptop of that hill and look down at Mama as she hung the wash or chopped wood or weeded the garden, waving and giggling at her every time she looked up at them, all the while them wondering what it would feel like, what would happen, if they were to vanish down the other side of the hill. Back then, Hank had never imagined standing on top of Mama's Hill and not being able to see his house.

He stared down the hill toward where the house should be, where he *knew* it stood, but couldn't see it for the shroud of smoke that covered it just as sure as each new, hungry year clouds memory and sunders the past. The smoke shifted and, for some seconds, he saw a window, the side door, before they disappeared again. Was it possible to get lost walking from the top of Mama's Hill to where he'd been born? He remembered crisp, cold mornings where it hurt your lungs good to take a deep breath, the early sun varnishing his mother's broad back as she lugged water from the well, stars sharp as sickles guarding his sleep. He hadn't expected those memories to be wrapped in a gauze of stinking smoke. But then he shrugged —that old Hunt's Station shrug, Job's shrug, of defeat and acceptance of defeat—shut his eyes, again conjured his mother's stooped boulder of a back, and scuffled down the hill.

His father had never been one to let things go. But the back door, gray, weather-warped, and out of true, bristled with splinters, had become as brittle as an old lady's hip. And the doorhandle, always painted an oily crow-black and sanded smooth, had gone to rust. Burred steel bit Hank's hand.

"Comin' in'r what?"

The voice edgy, burred as the doorhandle, a voice grown fed up with words years ago. To Lloyd Rodgers, thumbnailing a match to stoke his Lucky Strike was conversation enough; and someone paying attention could tell what he was thinking by how hard he struck that match.

Hank kept one picture of his old man in his wallet. In the black-and-white photo, Lloyd Rodgers is maybe twenty, strong and skinny like a crowbar, dressed in tight black jeans and a clean white T-shirt; he cradles five quarts of beer in his rugged arms, glares at the camera in a don't-screw-with-me pose; he wears a thick black belt, its buckle a clenched brass fist. It's the only picture Hank keeps of his father because it's the only one that even hints at his old man's truths, dents the surface of his rage. And that belt, that wicked, wicked belt, with its dulled brass fist, had licked Hank's ass more than a few times.

House reeked of stale cigarette smoke, flat beer, bacon grease. Hank's father sat at the kitchen table, drinking his breakfast beer, staring out the soot-silted window. He glanced up when Hank walked in.

"You come back," his father said.

Hank nodded, his father already stealing his words.

With a flick of his head, Lloyd Rodgers motioned to the chair at the other end of the table.

Hank sat down.

"Staying?" his father asked.

Hank squinted, furrowed his forehead.

"For good?" his father said.

"Don't know."

"Like hell."

Hank noticed the five-string banjo, his great-grandfather's Gibson, standing next the stove.

"Picking?"

"Some"—a gulp of beer—"enough."

"Too bad 'bout those empty houses."

"Water went bad . . . all their babies died . . . moved away." A pause. "You know the story." A rasping cough.

Hank stared hard at his father: his toothless mouth caved in . . . forehead and face a delta of wrinkles, gullies carved by inner floods . . . nose a little red and puffy, ever so slightly misshapen . . . just-shaved chin and cheeks raw . . . fingernails gnawed deep into their beds . . . hair slicked back and piled high, like some aging country singer's.

"Gone t'hell, ain't I?" He laughed, coughed again.

"You say so."

"Know so."

Hank shrugged.

His father looked at Hank's arms.

"Some accident, I heard."

"Fuckin' Dirty Willy."

"Y'okay?"

"Guess so."

His father took another drink of beer—WillyBrew.

"Hungry?"

"Could eat the asshole out of a skunk."

Another laugh, another cough, another drink.

After breakfast they walked up to Jerusalem Ridge, a hill north of Fire Town where three old fieldstone chimneys stood. The Chimneys were believed to date back to Revolutionary times, but no one knew for sure. And no one could remember ever hearing any stories about anyone living up there. Ever. To Hank those chimneys had always spoken of ruin and endurance, as present-day sentinels and witnesses to an unknowable past. Ultimately, their magic lay in the stones themselves, fissured glacier-borne ancients torn from the fields and now become somehow supernatural. Up on Jerusalem Ridge at The Chimneys, you could watch Fire Town's slow burn, consider the center of town, study Sanborn Hunt's devil work.

"Women come up here sometimes," Hank's father said. "Play their fiddles."

"I always liked it up here," Hank said.

"One of the old dead places . . . but there's more life here than in town. I got to sit."

The Angel Wind whipped across the hill, moaning through The Chimneys and riffling their hair. They sat up against the sun side of one of the chimneys.

"You going to move?" Hank asked his father.

"No. Lived there my whole life. Staying. Fire be damned . . . smoke be damned . . . everything be damned."

His eyes bore in on his son.

"This is the story, see. The ones who could leave, did. What's left is us who couldn't. I still make my money off Sanborn Hunt, I still get drunk off Dirty Willy's beer, and I still pass out in the house where I was born. That's just the way it's going to be.

"What I don't get is why the hell you come back."

3

Old Crow Can't Jump

Lives in Hunt's Station are spent in a ruthless present tense.

The past, that dried-up creek, carries no solace. And the future, the future waits somewhere beyond Raven's Roost, beyond The Crossroads. So . . . the seconds nip . . . the minutes gnaw . . . and the hours grind: toothy, rust-gutted gears that shriek and squeal in passing.

Spurned by sleep, Clare Hunt keeps watch on the front steps, stares down into the midnight town.

Her town, even come daybreak, is all shades of rain . . . night . . . sleep.

Seized by unholy flame, her town shrivels, wrinkles like a hand-rolled cigarette drooping from Dirty Willy Menard's splotchy, purple lips.

Her town's grief is not leavened by children, for there are no children here, where even the amniotic sac has become one of Sanborn Hunt's dark springs . . . where every woman is midwife to misery. There is no sudden laughter, no squalls of

25

tears, none of the ecstatic screeches born of the sheer joy at being ten, alive, and free.

Her town's roads narrow each year, forgotten arteries creeping from a withered heart.

Her town is all ravens and crows—gossiping, griping, scolding. Waiting.

Her town . . . all shades of rain . . . night . . . sleep. As is, she will sometimes admit, her heart.

Police Chief Styles Plectrum and Sanborn Hunt's foreman, Joe Bleak, face the night in Marian's Cafe, their crewcuts the color of cigarette smoke, playing checkers for a buck a game. Marian has long since escaped to bed. Some mornings, Styles and Joe are still there when she creaks downstairs to open, two, sometimes three, ashtrays full, their WillyBrew empties lined just so on the Formica counter—Joe's on the left, Styles's on the right.

"King me," Styles says.

Joe tilts back, fiddles with his belt, stretches, kneads the back of his red, creased neck, then moves.

Styles ambushes two more of Joe's checkers.

"Off your game, Joe."

"Screw."

"Still thinking about that Keegan kid?"

Joe shrugs.

"Hell of a thing."

"Factory ain't no place to get drunk. You know that better'n anybody."

"Christ, Sty, can the bullshit, huh? Who do you think you're talking to?"

The two men, cousins, practically brothers, born a week apart, stare at each other. Styles grins. Their voices rasp.

Joe says, "Someone fucking caved his head in, then shoved him in the lagoon. You know it. I know it. Everyone in this g.d. town knows it."

Styles's turn to shrug.

"You know how it is."

"You ain't the one found him."

They play on a cracker-thin cardboard checkerboard, beer-stained, cigarette-scarred, whose yellowed crinkling crease has been taped and retaped beyond counting; the red and black squares have gone to gray and pink from the nightly march of plastic checkers.

Joe plunges his fist into his dungarees pocket, fishes out a wadded-up dollar bill, hands it to Styles.

"Jesus, Joe, can't you carry a wallet like the rest of us?"

"Give it back, you so spleeny."

" 'Nother?"

Joe nods.

Bill Monroe and the Blue Grass Boys, their voices high, a haunting sorrow from the radio, tuned to WHWM, only station the town pulls in.

Joe turns up the radio.

"Boy, that Bill Monroe can sure give you the chills."

Styles nods, says, "Smoke before fire," and Joe moves his black checker, using just his index finger.

Styles counters.

Joe sighs.

"I just don't like it that someone went and killed that kid. Ain't right."

"Don't go getting started, Joe."

"Well, it ain't."

"Don't."

Joe lights another smoke, Styles opens another beer.

Styles says, "I'm sorry the kid's dead. But what I want to know is what the fuck he was doing here in the first place?"

Joe double-jumps and says, "King me."

Lloyd Rodgers and the dark keep each other company as Lloyd picks notes out of the night. He cradles his banjo, squirrels his fingers up and down the neck, plucks at the strings, searching, trying to latch onto that tune he knows is trembling at his fingertips. Tune always comes before the words. Always. He has written hundreds of songs. Songs that have kept him from being swallowed by the night, saved him from Sanborn Hunt's lagoon. But tonight, he knows, there will be no song—after all these years he can at least tell that much—and he plays, comforts himself with the first song he ever wrote, when he was just ten years old and in love with the banjo, when he dreamed about fleeing Hunt's Station and picking on the Grand Ole Opry: "Old Crow Can't Jump."

> Old Crow, Old Crow can't jump.
> Old Crow, just jigging on a stump.
> Up come a weasel, bit him on the rump.
> And that's the reason why
> Old Crow can't jump

Dirty Willy sounds deep into Hunt's Station, navigating mystery roads, snake roads, that only he remembers. Deep into woods where all of the animals—all of them, from black bears to deerflies—have either died or fled. Where whole stands of skeleton trees, bleached and stripped, guard roads that remain roads only through the force of Dirty Willy Menard's will. Where a dying town's sores and wounds never stop weeping. In the truck's bed the fifty-five-gallon steel drums mutter their poison lies, a heavy, metallic voice ever whispering to Willy. He snaps the radio on to the call and response of twin fiddles—ghost lovers. Dirty Willy mans WHWM for Sanborn Hunt too; he punched the tape loop before his poison run. Come midnight, he keeps the music as black and blue and bleak as he can: honky-tonk moaners, bluegrass so high and lonesome as to take your breath away, blues where each note is as sharp as a boning knife, and Hank Williams, always Hank, dead at twenty-nine, paining and pleading, blamed and bleeding, keening in a voice as stark as a serial killer whistling down a back road in the pouring rain. Dirty Willy backs the truck up to Lagoon No. 63, which had been West's Pond when he was a kid, grunts out, and rolls the steel drums into the black water; he doesn't have the patience tonight to crack each drum, drain it.

Maggie Parriss sits at her desk . . . chews on her pen. She's seventeen years old, almost eighteen, and, this fall, will be the only student from Hunt's Station at the regional high school in Miles' Grant. She has spent the night alone at The Chimneys; other nights there are friends, beer, boys. As this summer before her senior year passes, she has felt Hunt's Station try to weasel inside her, try to anchor her; she resists, keeps her head clear, by writing in her journal. She stares out her open window, catches a whiff from Fire Town—like the smell of a fresh-struck match—hears the shudder of a truck down-shifting deep in the woods.

Maggie Parriss uncaps her pen and writes: "I am the last child in Hunt's Station."

Hank Rodgers sleeps. He hasn't been back in town long enough not to.

4

Man of Constant Sorrow

"Don't see how you can stand living in a dead man's room like that."

"It isn't as if he died up there."

"Give me the willies."

"Well, I'm moving his stuff out after breakfast anyway."

Joe Bleak and Hank Rodgers sat eating in Marian's. They'd hid as far back as they could to get away from the Saturday-morning bacon-and-eggs crowd. An orange cat the size of a pillow snoozed in the sun-spattered window beside them.

"This restaurant hasn't changed since the day I left," Hank said. "I swear that cat was sleeping in that window the morning I drove off, fifteen years ago."

"Seems that way, don't it," Joe said. "Whole town seems that way. You got to look real close to see how things change."

"What do you mean?"

"Take Marian," said Joe, lighting up a Chesterfield. "She's

put on a good fifteen, twenty pounds, but folks don't notice because she's been coloring her hair. That mop of hers is blacker'n a crow's ass. And I'll tell you another thing, she ain't screwing Russell Hodge no more either. Won't even look at him when he's in here; makes one of the girls tend to him. Use to be, you couldn't even get Marian to blink at you when Russell had his fat ass planked in here."

Joe pulled on his cigarette, looked out the window.

"Way it is around here, no one sees what they don't want to see. You know that well as I do. Maybe you just forgot. Sanborn Hunt's been fucking this town up the ass for a good thirty years and everyone makes like nothing's happening—or worse, some of 'em acts like it feels good."

Joe, his eyes as dark and deep as one of Hunt's lagoons, stared at Hank.

"It don't make no sense for you to come back here, Hank. There ain't nothing here. It's all used up. We all sold our souls for the steel drum money, and now we're just waiting to shit the bed."

Hank poured more sugar into his coffee, stirred it, took a loud sip.

"I had to come back, Joe," he said. "I can't explain it, but I had to."

Joe scratched the cat's ears; the cat, Carl Perkins, purred but didn't budge. And Hank saw for the first time that Joe Bleak *had* changed. His chiseled face wasn't quite so sharp, had, like a gravestone from another century, been worn down, become home to cracks, fissures; his muscles were still ropy, but more like rope left outdoors too long, rope gone gray and brittle.

"Need help moving that kid's things?" Joe asked.

"Naw, that's all right," Hank said. "There's not that much. What was the story with that guy, anyway?"

"Just showed up one day—probably followed that stupid fucking Dirty Willy in—and didn't leave. Good worker, dependable. Never give me no trouble. I give him a couple raises. Some of 'em said he was writing a book on us, but I don't know nothing about that. And even if he was, more power to him."

"I can't believe he was fool enough to get crocked and fall in the lagoon. Christ."

"Who told you that?"

"Styles . . . my old man."

Joe shook his head, disgusted, mashed his cigarette out in the ashtray. "This friggin' town," he said. "This goddamned, cocksucking, sonuvabitching hole."

"What's the matter, Joe?"

"Hank, I'm the one that found Paul Keegan. And I'm the one pulled him out the lagoon. The back of that kid's head was stove up 'bout the same as the front of your car after you smacked into Dirty Willy. Paul Keegan didn't die from no drowning in no goddamned lagoon."

"But . . ."

"Someone killed him, Hank, then treated him like he was no better than some fifty-five-gallon sack of shit."

"They murdered this guy?"

Joe nodded.

"How come no one called in the State Police or the county?"

Joe looked at Hank like he was simple.

"When do you think the last time was a statie come sniffing around here?"

Hank shrugged.

"What they do with the body?"

"For all I know," Joe Bleak said, "they put Paul Keegan back right where I found him."

Hank had most of Keegan moved out and down in Marian's cellar by noon: the fax machine, the cellular phone, the Apple Macintosh LC II, the color TV (Hank hadn't come back home to watch no g.d. TV), the work clothes (smelling of sweat, WillyBrew, and insecticide), the VCR, the tweed blazer and Timberland shoes. The only bits of Keegan left in the room were five books (*Up in the Old Hotel* by Joseph Mitchell, short story collections by Hemingway and Ward Just, and two collections of Faulkner's novels, 1930–1935 and 1936–1940, published by the Library of America), a shoebox stuffed with 1967 Topps baseball cards, and a manuscript stacked and centered on the table by the window like some 500-page doily.

Hank shivered in the room's emptiness, and he suddenly missed his wife. Not even her, really, but her presence, her heat, the space she filled.

His marriage hadn't been bad, he supposed; he just hadn't understood it. He couldn't remember the transitions between meeting this woman, dating her, sleeping with her, living with her, and then marrying her. It wasn't clear to him how it had happened. So, neither happy nor unhappy, they had lived in Manhattan, nurtured their careers (career, my ass, he thought, backup spokesman for Puritan Chemical Products), nurtured their friends, ate out too much, saw films (God forbid that they should merely go to the movies), traveled some (Paris, Santa Fe, Toronto), shared the *Times* at breakfast, fucked each other much harder than necessary at night, and called it being married. Still, a part of Hank had always been detached, on guard—back in Hunt's Station. And his wife, a smart woman, knew this and finally resented it. And he didn't blame her. But she had wanted him so badly at the beginning—maybe misinterpreting his deep silences as strength—and, flattered, he had simply acquiesced. He hadn't changed; she just hadn't seen.

He shivered again.

Keegan's manuscript, the last words of a dead and disappeared man, troubled Hank. He kept his distance, stood in the middle of the room, the way you would with a growling dog or a cantankerous drunk. He considered hiding it, though he didn't know why, and he considered burning it. But, most of of all, he wanted to read it. WillyBrew in hand, he crept up to the table, slid into a chair, and pulled the manuscript, *The Dirtiest Town in America,* toward him and read the first paragraph:

Dark currents rage across this country—New Aryans, serial killers, rock 'n' roll Messiahs—currents invisible to see, impossible currents, until they swirl into your neighborhood, suck under someone you love. By chance—and maybe just sheer bad luck—I followed one such small black tributary and found a desolate town both ruled and ruined by one old man. His name is Sanborn Hunt. And he is the only genuinely evil man I have ever met.

Hank read the paragraph three more times, slower each time, moving his lips, squinting, jaw muscles bunched. Then he shoved himself away from the table like a man who is full, jumped up, and ran out the door.

After a sneaky-cool morning, Saturday afternoon broke hot and muggy. And in that sleepy hour after lunch thick

August heat, like a chenille bedspread soaked in lukewarm water, blanketed the town. An empty Main Street shimmered in the sun: the ancient cats and dogs drowsed, on porch railings, under steps, in alleys, twitchy in their animal dreams; Marian, humming Patsy Cline's "Crazy," cleaned her restaurant as if she had the whole day to get the job done; Styles Plectrum, hat saving his eyes, dozed on the bench in front of the barber shop; even the crows and ravens were quiet in the cool, dark woods.

But by about three o'clock the town began to fill, the men heading for Tater Tate's Tavern or the firehouse, while the women homed in on Bev's Beauty Boutique or Hempel's Grocery; both women and men poked around Ken Meyer's hardware store. Saws whined and hammers whapped as the town crew set up the stage at the Hunt Waste Management edge of Main Street. Front porches became hives of laughter and gossip, while a certain kind of man sat stonily on the Town Hall steps, smoking, squinting into the sun. Instrument cases leaned in doorways, hung off arms, tilted on benches.

Hiding in his office now, then back to the street, Styles Plectrum wondered which of his friends had killed Paul Keegan—and what he could do about it if he found out. They were all used to death and dying in Hunt's Station, from Sanborn Hunt's grind, or the demons that drove men to flames on The Whispering Turnpike, or sucking on a shotgun. But murder, that was too forthright for a town like Hunt's Station.

As she watched Main Street come to life, like some parched patch of desert after a rainstorm, Clare Hunt was tempted to leave her father's house, the house he refused to set foot in anymore and which she refused to set foot out of, and prepare for that night's singing. But she feared that once she stepped through that front door, walked down those red-brick steps, and left her father's property, she might do something she'd regret—though she had no idea what that might be. She sighed. She would just have to be satisfied with going up to the roof, to the widow's walk, as she did every Saturday night and listen to the singing from up there. It was a relief and a joy to just listen.

Banjo slung over his back, Lloyd Rodgers haunted the shadows where the woods and the center of town couldn't quite decide who belonged to what and what belonged to who. He'd always felt most at home in those shadows, recognizable but unknowable, and that was one of the reasons he'd stayed in Fire Town. His music flowed from those shadows. Stick him on some sun-drenched hillside and tell him to write a song, and all he'd end up doing was fall asleep or stare at the sky. But strand him among the shadows, leave him in the deep woods, abandon him to the crying hours after midnight but before sunrise and the songs wouldn't stop; his music had always flowed as black as the waters beneath Hunt's Station. Lloyd wouldn't have minded a beer, but he had no patience for the drinkers at Tate's Tavern; he would have liked nothing better than to curl up in a dark corner of the bar with a beer or two and his banjo, but once he walked in they'd start jabbering at him about the good old days and the bad old days and every goddamned thing in between. He was too old for that shit. His wife had died too soon, his town was poison, and his only boy had run off for fifteen years. A man who acknowledged those things, who tried to understand them, who had let that sorrow become part of his marrow, didn't suffer the fools he'd known from day one at Tater Tate's Tavern.

He coughed, lit a cigarette, and slouched against a tree;

within five minutes he had the banjo out and was picking at a new song.

Hank had put on fresh-washed dungarees and a clean white dress shirt; he'd also flung Keegan's manuscript into the bread box. As he got ready for the singing, he felt that nervous wobble in his stomach that he hadn't felt since he was a kid going out with Clare Hunt. He had never had the gut-flutters over his wife; back then he had chalked it up to maturity; he knew better now.

Ever since he could remember, he had loved the singings, which were never over until each and every person who wanted to play or sing had taken the stage; there had once been a singing, his father told him, that had lasted six days solid.

His mother had loved the singings, too, had lived for putting on one of her ankle-dusting cotton dresses and herding Hank and his sisters, Alison and Iris, into town on a Saturday afternoon. They'd never seen Lloyd on a Saturday until he took the stage that night. Hank's father was the star and—on Saturdays anyway—he acted the part.

His mother had always sung when they were kids: "I'll Meet You in Church on Sunday Morning" and "Let Me Walk Lord by Your Side" and "Mary Had a Little Lamb" whisked right in with songs by Kitty Wells, Loretta Lynn, and Patsy Cline. And if she wasn't singing, she had the radio tuned to WHWM or had the record-player humming. The music, Hank realized now, had helped lighten her days. Hanging the wash when it was ten below wasn't quite so bad if you had Loretta Lynn to keep you company. And chopping wood was almost like going to church if you saw it as chance to go hymning.

In the end, as she died her Hunt's Station death, it seemed as if the music was the only thing that kept her alive. As she came and went, wandering that wilderness between here and after, she hummed and sang and hymned, her musical moans filling not just the house but all Fire Town. They moved the record-player into her room and she died listening to "Keep on the Sunny Side" by the Carter Family.

Tears ambushed Hank, and he once again saw his mother, shriveled to a fetal curl, shivering in her deathbed even though the temperature had hit 101 degrees that day . . . Alison and Iris changing the records . . . his father, a faltering shadow in the doorway.

In summer, in that hour after the sun has drowned in the West but before night reigns, the blood quickens at the music of the coming darkness, the air trembles. The day's heat is shrugged off, peeled away. The night cool beckons.

It is the hour of children's last desperate whoops and hollers as they dart up and down alleys, in and out of shadows, like bats—and in Hunt's Station, where there are no more children, memories of those joyful cries fill that hour, and if you listen hard enough with your head cocked just so, it seems as if the children never left. It is the hour to yearn for the night and its secrets, or to flinch at its truths; the hour when the day just past is shaped into memory and the coming night is dreamed; the hour of preparation, anticipation, when that certain supper cooking on the stove is meant as a kind of seduction; the hour of perfume and after-shave, of shined shoes and hair worried one hundred strokes, of starch-stiff shirts and soft cotton dresses; the hour of counting your money and your blessings, of cinching the belt one more notch and, hands on hips, staring down the mirror till it shows you what you want to—need to—see.

A slow hour, a lovers' hour, as night and day waltz toward night's black door where day will lift her chin and surrender. And in August it's an hour, too, for the uninvited shiver as the air suddenly cools and autumn whispers cold in your ear like a long-dead love.

It was in the last minutes of this hour that Hunt's Stationers gathered at the end of Main Street for the singing. Lugging instrument cases, their hampers stuffed with ham-and-cucumber sandwiches, yellow slabs of smoked cheddar, jars of pickles, olives, and cauliflower, and jumbo bags of potato chips, they roosted on blankets and folding chairs on porches and rooves, in the trees and atop the pickup trucks as Dirty Willy, parked at the very back of the crowd, sold beer out the trunk of his '67 Dodge Dart.

Hunt's Station had no town meetings, no school board meetings, no planning board meetings. There was no historical society or library committee or Lions Club or Rotary. There was work and the singings, and in between you had to figure it out for yourself.

When the lights came up on the spare, dark stage, everyone clapped as Joe Bleak strode from the shadows; they clapped as much for themselves as for Joe.

Joe wore straight-legged dungarees stiff with newness, a crisp white shirt bragging red-and-black stitching across the chest as fine and sharp as December rain, and a black string tie with a turquoise-and-silver clasp. He was also barefoot.

"The whole week I got to wear my workingman's boots," he'd say. "On Saturday night, I like to let my feet breathe."

His voice as deep as a good well, Joe spoke into the microphone.

"Thank you, everybody, thank you. It's sure nice to see you all out here tonight, and I know we're going to have our usual fine show, 'cause you folks wouldn't have it any other way."

Standing tiptoe, he sniffed the air, tilted his head toward Fire Town.

"Either Fire Town's a mite strong tonight or Brother Lloyd Rodgers forgot to turn off the iron 'fore he left the house."

They laughed, a friendly and knowing laughter leavened with a we're-all-in-this-together sobriety.

Joe smiled. "Anyway, folks, I know we got a dandy show ahead. We got us a new singer tonight—I ain't telling right yet who it is—and Brother Lloyd promised me a couple new songs to go with the other *ten thousand or so* he's already wrote." Joe rolled his eyes—"As if we needed a couple more"—and they laughed again.

"But before we move on . . . I got me a new song myself."

The crowd hooted and clapped. Joe Bleak could sing and write pretty good, but he couldn't pick guitar to save his soul.

Hunched on a stool and playing guitar like chopping wood, Joe banged time with his left foot, thunked out some basic blues chords, and growled up his voice: "This here's 'The Dirty Willy Blues.'" (And Dirty Willy looked up from his cashbox.)

Dirty Willy, he crawls round
in that beer-makin' sin.
Dirty Willy, he scratches round
in that beer-makin' sin.
But, Dirty Willy, man, just what
kinda hops you been squirtin' in?

(The crowd gasped, cackled in appreciation, and looked back
at Dirty Willy, who wasn't smiling one damn bit. A couple of
the men looked at Joe Bleak, looked at Dirty Willy, looked at
their bottles of beer, then poured their WillyBrew on the
ground.)

That Dirty Willy, y'know he smells
like your great-grandma's thing.
That Dirty Willy, y'know he reeks
like your great-granny's thing.
But Dirty Willy, yeah he's the slimy snake
what makes your little heifer sing.

(Roaring now, maybe trying to hee-haw away all of the past
week's poisons—hell, maybe the whole past month's—the
crowd couldn't stop. Keeping a straight face, eyes closed, Joe
thumped it out. Dirty Willy slammed his cashbox shut and
started slinking toward the stage, sharpening his black eyes on
Joe Bleak, a pickaxe in his hand.)

Dirty Willy, you know he's been
slopping Sanborn Hunt's hog.
Dirty Willy, you know he's the man been
slopping Sanborn's big ol' hog.
Now Dirty Willy, good people, keep him
away from your fine bitch dog.

Wordless, chest heaving, Dirty Willy vaulted onto the stage and charged Joe Bleak. Some of them swore later that they saw Dirty Willy devolve when he jumped onto that stage, saw him shudder into some kind of wer-weasel or wer-skunk, turn into his true self. And even later some of them realized that even though Willy Menard had been in town for as long as anyone could recall, no one remembered him ever being a child.

Willy brought the pickaxe back over his head, his pale, hairy gut mooning out from under his shirt, and swung down at Joe, who rolled under and away from the blow. Leaving the pick stuck in the stage, Willy yowled and jumped Joe, who was laughing.

"Don't you laugh at me, you cocksucker," Willy snarled. "Don't you never."

"Get bent, pussle-gut."

Joe shrugged Willy off, the way a snake sheds its skin, stood him up, booted him in the ass, and sent him flailing down the stage steps. When Willy, howling now, tried to scramble back, Hank Rodgers pulled him down from behind, making sure Willy smacked his head a good one on the ground, and waited for Styles Plectrum to cart Willy off to Hunt's Station's one jail cell. As Willy lay there, gasping and flopping, his eyes rolling up in his head, Hank remembered his car accident and kicked Willy a couple good ones in the ribs out of pure Hunt's Station spite.

It was good to be back home.

Willy gone, the crowd settled into a lazy buzz. Joe Bleak, still smiling, came back on stage and shook his head.

"Now there's a man takes his blues serious," he said,

toeing at the pickaxe still stuck in the stage. "Course, he never could pick worth a lick."

The crowd, still with him, laughed.

"By the way, tonight all the beer's on Willy."

Hank parked himself at Dirty Willy's Dart, dispensing free beer and details about his car accident and news about his past fifteen years. Most Hunt's Stationers stuck to the beer and Hank's crash; they knew all they wanted to know about the past fifteen years in Hunt's Station, and since Hank Rodgers hadn't been a part of it, they didn't really care where he'd holed himself up.

Traitors are allowed to come back home, but just don't go rubbing anyone's nose in it. So they said they didn't care about Hank Rodgers and the Big City—or, at least, pretended not to care.

All except one. All except Maggie Parriss.

5

Wake Up, Little Maggie

"Ladies and gentlemen, little Maggie Parriss."

Polite applause, the first notes of a spring shower. Maggie walked toward the microphone, swaying, walking the way a body does toward the dunking preacher at a river baptism. The guitar, blond and plain, looking too big for her. Looking as if it spent more time banging off her bony hips and knobby knees than bending to her musical will. But no one said anything. They'd all learned a long time ago not to say anything.

"First time I've ever been up here," Maggie said. "Guess you know that already. But I've got me some things . . . some things I've got to sing."

Maggie looked out into the crowd—family, neighbors, distant relations, but no friends, really. She'd somehow sprouted in this poison Hunt's Station soil and, without much water and just a bit of shade, had thrived; which wasn't to say she was happy. Yes, she was smart and she was good-looking. But happy? Happy people in Hunt's Station were either simple or hiding something. She smiled to herself.

"This song," Maggie Parriss said, "is called 'The Last Child.'"

> I am the last child.
> I am the last child.
> The days make me too sad.
> And my nights are too wild.
>
> The boys and the men started
> at me when I was just ten.
> The boys and the men started
> at me when I was barely ten.
> 'Cause I'm the last child.
> All because I'm the last child.
> The last child.
>
> I grew up with no brothers.
> I grew up with no sisters.
> I grew up with no friends.
> All I had was my soul-searching blisters.
> I am the last child.
> I am the last child.
> Because I'm the last child.
> All because I'm the last child.
> Last child.

The women wept.

Men stared down into their beer.

Maggie cried too, almost hadn't been able to finish. It'd been the first time she'd truly sung the song, and it had ambushed her, its unsuspected strength nearly overwhelming her.

Her people's sob-pierced silence meant more to her than any amount of clapping and hooting could have. She had ripped out their hearts, then made them look.

The stage blinked dark and Joe Bleak led Maggie off, his heavy hands light on her skinny shoulders, a father guiding a sleepwalking child back to bed. He didn't say anything. She knew what she had done, he knew what she had done, and so did the rest of Hunt's Station. No reason to speak. Didn't have the words, anyway.

None of them did.

Maggie drifted back toward the beer, toward Hank Rodgers. She saw Hank's father, Lloyd, tucked in the shadows of an oak tree, thought he had winked at her. She shrugged, made for Dirty Willy's Dodge Dart. *Dirty Willy* . . . she shook her head. And as she walked, as she thought about what she had just done, there was a melting in her usually tight chest, her ears prickled, her cheeks flushed. It was as if seventeen years of ice, glacier-thick ice, was going out, breaking up into iceberg-size chunks and bobbing away from Hunt's Station. And it was in that moment, as her step lightened, as she felt summer and desire crawl deep, then deeper, inside her, that she knew she would leave Hunt's Station, that nothing could keep her there.

She had sung the truth. She had broken the chains.

"Maggie Parriss," said Hank Rodgers, handing her a beer. "I remember the year you were born. Yours was the only name listed in the Town Report under births."

She smiled. Her parents had kept that Town Report, her name, Margaret Nanci Parriss, lonely in eight-point type on the otherwise blank, white page.

"So, what's New York City like?" she asked Hank. "What's it really like?"

She tilted her head back and took a long swallow of beer, and Hank found himself staring at, aching for, the past: a girl, a young woman, in cutoffs and a man's workshirt, drinking a beer, thinking escape, pining for the freedom beyond The Crossroads.

"Well," Hank said, "the most important thing about New York City is that it's not here."

"Yeah," she said. "Don't think I don't know that."

"Now I'm not saying that's good or bad."

"Anywhere has to be better than Hunt's Station. Just anywhere."

"Maybe so. But I'm back, ain't I?"

And Maggie Parriss, suddenly some kind of Hunt's Station star, and the beer already surging in her head, looked Hank right in the eye and said, "Well, they always said you was fucking crazy."

She laughed. He smiled. She flounced down next to him on the Dart's scabby back bumper. She took another beer. Hank too.

"That was some song you sang, Maggie Parriss," Hank said.

"Uh-huh," said Maggie, meaning that she didn't want to talk about it.

They watched Those G.D. Crows—Gib Crow and his four sons—do a couple of Flatt and Scruggs numbers: "Flint Hill Special" and "I'm Head Over Heels in Love With You."

"Sound good as they always did," Hank said. "I tell ya, they could make a living out there."

"Don't want to leave," Maggie said. "I know those Crow boys, and that old Mr. Gib raised them just as stubborn as he is. They'll choke and die here in this damn place. Smile doing it."

"You can't wait to get out, can you?"

"What do you think?"

Hank shook his head. "I was just like you, Maggie," he said. "That morning I took off I would've rathered jumped in one of old Sanborn's lagoons and drowned than stay one more day."

"Yut."

Those G.D. Crows were walloping away at "Old Crow Can't Jump" now, each Crow flapping and flopping up and down during his solo.

"That's one of your Dad's songs, ain't it?" Maggie asked.

"Yut," Hank said. "First one he ever wrote. He was just ten years old."

"Ever go up there? On the stage?"

"Just to help out my old man. Play some guitar, some mandolin."

"Ever write?"

"No songs. I sure wasn't going to try and compete with my old man. I wrote poems, stories, high school shit. I was going to go away and become some bigshot writer."

"What happened?"

Hank stared at Maggie the way a drunk stares in the mirror at three in the morning.

"I don't know."

He opened another beer, looking away now.

"I guess . . . I guess I didn't want it bad enough. After I got away from Hunt's Station, I never wanted nothing bad enough. It was like getting out of this hole had used up everything I had."

By just looking at him, sitting next to him, Maggie felt freer than she ever had. Here was a man, a native Hunt's Stationer, who had left for fifteen years. Maybe his sorry return was a sign that she should just go, go as soon as she could.

"You want to go for a ride, Maggie Parriss?"

"Yes. Yes I do, Hank Rodgers."

Come midnight, Lloyd Rodgers had already been playing for a good hour and showed no sign of letting up, like a good rain, a farmer's rain. In tight black jeans and tight white T-shirt, Lloyd sat on his stool and picked and sang; his daughters backed him, Alison and Iris on twin fiddles, and anyone who felt moved to could go on up and play guitar. Eyes shut, barely acknowledging the crowd, Lloyd burrowed into his music, his banjo as much a digging tool as a musical instrument. Six days a week this town was run by Sanborn Hunt. On Saturday night, it belonged to Lloyd Rodgers.

Lloyd and his girls finished up "Bury My Bones 'neath Raven's Roost," and as Hunt's Station clapped, Lloyd hollered back to his daughters, "Hunt's Hill Hobo!"

> Run, hobo, run.
> Run, hobo, run.
> Can't stay in this town.
> The hounds'll tear you down.
> So run, hobo, run.
> Run, hobo, run.

Lloyd's voice high as Hunt's Hill, lyrics tumbling out, Alison and Iris harmonizing behind their father, knowing the exact places to fill behind Lloyd's thin voice as only members of the same family can. Lloyd slammed into his solo, banjo breaknecking after that hapless hobo, that filthy Hunt's Hill hobo. And those who closed their eyes could see that hobo, scrabbling over fences, staggering down Main Street, stumbling into the dark woods, chased by Lloyd Rodgers' banjo, Lloyd's music-upped hounds, snarling and snapping and howling.

> Dead, hobo, dead.
> Dead, hobo, dead.
> Couldn't live in this town.
> Those ol' hounds run him down.
> So dead, hobo, dead.
> We . . . already . . . dug . . . your . . . bed.

Clare Hunt, nesting in the shadow-washed frontroom, half-listening to the singing through the open window, Maggie Parriss's song still sobbing in her head. Both the song and Maggie's sweet, clear voice have haunted her all night. Maggie's song a pebble still rippling in Clare's small pond. Clare, curled there in the musty dark, whispers: "I am the last child. I am the last child. I am the last child."

Styles Plectrum considered Dirty Willy, asleep in the jail cell. Dirty Willy, whose loamy root face wasn't even softened by sleep, looking like something you'd find in one of Sanborn Hunt's fifty-five-gallon steel drums. Dirty Willy, who had long ago accepted what all of them had become in Hunt's Station, and had even reveled in it.

"Did you do it, Willy?" Styles asked. "Did you kill that

Keegan kid? Or was it somebody else? Was it Marian? Or Gib Crow? Or even ol' Sanborn himself? What do you say, Willy? What do you think?"

No sound from the cot. Styles sighed and headed out the door to listen to Lloyd.

"Or was it me?" he asked himself.

Hank and Maggie sounded deep into Hunt's Station, slinking down shadow paths and half roads. But even so, miles from Main Street, they could hear the banjo bark and the fiddles moan, and all Maggie Parriss could say, could demand, was "Just do it, okay? Just fuck me," and they fell asleep in Dirty Willy's Dodge Dart, entangled.

Lloyd Rodgers is still playing as the sun rises. His voice rasped out hours ago . . . finger skin flaps and finger blood sprays . . . his arms throb . . . and still he plays, plays his grandfather's banjo. He picks faster and faster and faster, as if trying to outrun a freight train, then slows, plucking notes out of the last of the night, notes as brittle as December leaves, music black and bleak and blue . . . blackgrass . . . music trying, maybe, to call down the fury of God. Lloyd's eyes deep and haunted, cheekbones keen, chin stubbled like a November cornfield. Lloyd Rodgers, suffused with his music and wracked by it, the fuse surrendering itself. His audience a handful of the stone-faced men, filterless cigarettes and black coffee, blunt brick hands, stagnant eyes. Men like Lloyd Rodgers . . . and Joe Bleak . . . Hunt's Station men . . . doomed men . . . as the banjo strings peel Lloyd's fingers . . . layer by layer by layer.

6

The Walls of Time

"Y'old man was somethin' Sat'dy night," Joe Bleak said to Hank Rodgers. "Ain't seen him pick like that since before when."

"Blood music," said Styles Plectrum, shaking his head in pleasure like he'd just polished off a good Sunday dinner. "Ain't no one plays the blood music, that good, deep marrow music, no more except Lloyd Rodgers."

Hank nodded.

"Heard he was real good."

Joe and Styles grinned. Marian poured coffee.

"Yeah, we heard about *that*, too," Joe said. "So . . . she sing for ya?"

Hank blushed. Here he was, thirty-goddamned-two, and Joe Bleak and Styles Plectrum could still redden him up like he was some kid starting out up the factory.

"Jesus, Hank, her old man asked me if you was planning on marrying her or something," Styles said. "But I stuck up for ya. Said a fine boy like you couldn't help but do the right thing."

The two men laughed.

"Screw you guys."

Joe stoked a Chesterfield, Styles a Camel.

"And what do you suppose Clare Hunt's going to think?" said Joe, working the needle deeper . . . past funny. "Here you ain't even gone to see her yet, and you're already jumping and pumping something else. And, Christ, in Dirty Willy's Dart, yet."

Joe stared Hank down. He'd given his joke half a turn and shamed Hank with it. Worse, Hank knew he was right to do it.

"That song a Maggie's sure tore us up," Styles said. "Reminded me of when Clare was a kid."

Joe freed Hank from his snare. "When I helped her off the stage, I swear I could feel her heart thumping all the way up her shoulders."

The two older men let Hank come up for air and they all lapsed into breakfasty silence: knife scraping toast, the tink of fork on plate, coffee sipped and slurped, ketchup burped onto homefries, the crunch of bacon. Sounds of contentment. Sounds that, many mornings, passed for conversation.

"When you letting Willy out?" Hank asked Styles.

"This morning. No point making a man miss a day's work."

"He was something pissed Sat'dy night," Hank said.

Joe shrugged. "You know, I'm fucking sick of Dirty Willy Menard. Fucking sick of that guy. Acts like he's the son-ta-bitch runs this town. But you know what? Sanbord Hunt owns the sweat on his balls, just like he does the rest of us."

"Know what ticks me?" Styles said. "Thinks he's something special 'cause he does so much of the drum hauling, 'cause he's the one helped Sanborn screw this town."

"And it don't bother him," Joe said. "Don't bother the cold cocksucker a-tall."

"Well," Hank said, "I still say he made me crash into his truck on purpose. Bastard."

Joe and Styles shrugged.

"I tell ya," Hank said. "The other night, when I had him down on the ground, I wanted to kick his teeth out his asshole."

Joe smiled. "Yeah, I saw you massaging his ribs with your size ten. Still got that old Hunt's Station rat snarling in your heart, huh, son?"

"That'd explain a lot," Styles said. "Whole hell of a lot."

"Guess I do," Hank Rodgers sighed. "Guess I goddamned do."

The note lay on Hank's table when he got back from breakfast, written on thick paper the color of straw. Kind of paper that sops up ink and whose grainy surface reminds you that paper's squeezed from trees. Kind of paper where your pen shudders over the fibers like driving on dirt-road washboard.

The note read:
HANK R
LETS TALK
      SH

The air smelled like snakes. A low, gray sky made people hunch over like they were grubbing in the root cellar for last year's turnips. Gates screaked . . . windows quivered . . . the lukewarm wind spit dirt. Mugginess clung to the town—a low-grade fever.

"Suicide weather," Hank's father used to say. "Day like this—may's well kill yourself 'fore somebody else does it for ya."

Then he'd laugh. That Hunt's Station sense of humor.

As Hank walked toward Hunt Waste Management he didn't think much about Sanborn Hunt's summons—old Sanborn meant nothing to him anymore—but instead worried on Paul Keegan and his manuscript. Hank wondered what could have drawn a rank stranger to Hunt's Station. What did an outsider's eyes see?

Even though Hank'd been gone fifteen years, he still couldn't step back and see Hunt's Station whole. His Manhattan friends had told him stories about going back home, about how their parents spoke with accents, how the towns where they'd grown up seemed no more than elaborate movie sets. But for Hank, Hunt's Station was blood. And with blood there's no detachment, only the search for, and satisfaction with, like blood. Hank heard no accents, he only heard the rush of blood.

Still, what had Keegan seen? What had he done to be killed? Hank wanted to read Keegan's manuscript, but its first paragraph had scared him, shamed him. Had Hank's people been so greedy and so weak as to let Sanborn Hunt's puny evil damn them?

More than anything, Sanborn Hunt's sovereignty embarrassed Hank.

He stopped, kneaded his right calf with his knuckles; a

knot the size of a silver dollar, a last souvenir from his car accident, gnawed at the muscle. Stump-sitting, he rolled up his pant leg and drove his knuckles into the gristly knot; the calf seized up like an oil-starved engine.

"Goddammit!"

So, he stumped there by the side of the road, waiting for the calf to loosen. When Dirty Willy mumbled by and asked him if he wanted a ride, Hank Rodgers told him to go fuck himself.

Sanborn Hunt's trailer, warped, rust-rabid, reflecting its owner's true self, squatted on a knoll overlooking Hunt Waste Management. Sanborn hardly ever went down the hill anymore. He ran his business from up the trailer; those who needed to speak with him were obliged to make the steep trudge up.

Sanborn, cigarette wagging from his mouth, wobbled out the trailer barechested, swayed on the front steps, unbuttoned his fly, took a leak, then stumbled back inside.

Hank stopped at the entrance to Hunt Waste Management. He realized he had never passed through those rusted gates without his father. He'd spent three summers working with his old man at HWM, three summers learning to massage poison: shipping it and receiving it, burning it and burying it, dumping it and then dumping it again. Thousands upon thousands of fifty-five-gallon steel drums, skull-and-crossbones stickers leering, brimming with liquid poisons; each steel drum bringing more money—and more death—to Hunt's Station.

None of them had ever stopped to think about it, the unspoken pact they had made with Sanborn Hunt. He had simply come back to Hunt's Station one day bearing jobs and money, and no one had asked questions. And by the time there were questions to ask, they weren't worth asking.

Standing at the gates, Hank thought about his father and Joe Bleak and all the other men grayed and hollowed by this job, by Sanborn Hunt's nightmare. With his money and his poison, Sanborn had turned those men to husks, given them lives as gaunt and brittle as November stalks. Hank couldn't imagine what Sanborn Hunt wanted. And he realized he'd responded to the old man's summons out of some unthinking communal habit.

The wind blew harder and the sky seemed to drop even lower, low enough even to worry the tallest trees. Hank pictured old Sanborn skulking about his trailer, one crabbed hand cranking a wind machine, the other gripping a lever that raised and lowered the sky—like Vincent Price in some old horror movie.

Hank turned around and limped back toward town.

From his steps, Sanborn Hunt watched Hank Rodgers turn back. He smiled his crafty old vulture smile. He'd corner Lloyd Rodgers' son soon enough.

Then Sanborn Hunt grunted up from the steps and surveyed his empire—that moonscape pocked by thousands of poison-packed fifty-five-gallon steel drums—and nodded. Nodded the way a man does on Sunday morning when the preacher's got his ears prickling with the Spirit.

"Yut," said Sanborn Hunt, almost proud, still nodding. "Yut. This here Mr. Hank Fucking Rodgers is the g.d. asshole of the twentieth century."

———

Clare Hunt placed what she needed on the table next to her bed: the square of gauze snugged to a right angle, liquid soap, powder, alcohol swab, and a small enamel basin filled with warm water. She pulled the shades shut, leaving one window open a crack to let the wind writhe into the room. She propped two pillows against the bed's headboard, stripped, got into the bed, and leaned back into the pillows.

To the right of her navel, a tan plastic pouch, ten inches long, hung from her stomach. Her large intestine had been cut out, and in the colon's place, she joked to herself, she wore a glorified Baggie.

When she'd been sickest, when the bleeding wouldn't stop and she had needed a unit of blood a day, when the colitis had gnawed at her guts the way rust chews up the rocker panels on an old Chevy, the doctor had snaked a scope inside her and let her look: her colon was on fire. Just beneath the surface of her stomach flames raged orange and red. It looked like lava was coursing through her bowels. After she saw, Clare agreed to the surgery.

She slid a four-inch-by-four-inch adhesive wafer out of its package and set it on the bed alongside a fresh plastic pouch; the wafer had a hole cut in the center of it one inch by one and one-quarter inches. She snapped the pouch to the wafer to check the fit, then uncoupled them. She peeled the paper from the back of the wafer, exposing a tacky plastic; she then circled the opening on the back of the wafer with another strip of adhesive.

Clare didn't rush, each movement deliberate, fraught with memory. Once a week she changed her bag, and she used that changing to remember her three months in the hospital and how she had nearly died her Hunt's Station death. She had no doubts that Hunt's Station—her father and his devil's business, really—had somehow made her body turn on itself, had tricked her immune system into devouring her colon, and her along with it. She shrugged. Sooner or later, we're all double-crossed by our bodies. Her betrayal had just come sooner.

If you can survive it essentially whole, nearly dying in your twenties isn't such a bad lesson, Clare had decided. Time stops. The walls of time fall away, and you can see the past complete. Each moment in the present grows, takes on weight. The illness, the November rustling of Death's robes, magnifies the moment, and for the first time since childhood there's room not only to live in the moment but to move around in it, to try it on for size. Time is still a river, but it's frozen. And each day seems as endless as a ten-year-old's August.

In the wind-whispering silence of her bedroom, Clare remembered the stillness of her sickness, of waking at six and dragging her chair into the shaft of sunlight slanting into the room, then sighing into the chair, closing her eyes, and letting the dawn varnish her dying woman's blues.

But most often, when she thinks of her stay in the hospital, it's two in the morning: propped in her bed at the hospital, she cannot sleep; sleep has become an old friend she has lost track of, a friend who hasn't written in years. She listens to the plop-drop of her IV. Three liquids, on a superhighway of tubing, dribble into her veins: one liquid is clear, one is piss-green, and the last is as white and thick as heavy cream. Her aching arms are black and blue; her veins are wearing out. Each afternoon a nurse wraps Clare's arms in hot, wet towels, and the healing humidity about puts her to sleep. Her stomach rumbles. Sometimes a tremor from her dying colon, other times simple hunger. As the doctors try to rest her wracked and weary colon, she hasn't been allowed to eat for weeks and she can only take ice chips by mouth; she's become a fool for ice chips. A nurse out in the hall shouts "Keys!" and a great fist of keys sings along the tile floor. The clatter of their passing sets off a chorus of moans, gasps, and pleas on the ward; an old man's matter-of-fact voice chants: "I'm dying . . . I'm dying . . . I'm dying."

Claire feels the pressure build in her stomach, a pressure she has lived with in lesser and greater degrees for more than two years, and she swings herself up into sitting position, her bare feet flat on the cold, gritty floor. She shivers. Clutching the IV pole, she catches her breath, then shuffles toward the bathroom, she panting and the pole rattling like some Dickensian ghost. Her stomach clenches, relaxes, clenches again, and the pressure bears down. She and the IV pole, her skinny, noisy shadow, bump into the bathroom, the three bottles clinking in a perverse toast, and Clare slumps onto the toilet and lets go. For the twenty-fifth time that day blood and tissue stream from her body—she has already used twenty-three units of blood—as she doubles over. Sweat beads on her forehead; her eyes sting. She can't keep herself from looking in the mirror as she leaves the bathroom: her eyes sink deeper into her skull each day and her skin has become as fine and gray as the nest of a paper wasp.

Remembering those dying nights, Clare shook her head. She unsnapped the old bag, a couple of pinprick holes patched by Band-Aids, then peeled the wafer from her stomach. She dipped a gauze pad in the basin of warm water, squirted soap on it, then washed the just-exposed skin, brisk and purposeful—the way you wash a child or a dog.

The square of skin beneath the wafer was smooth and pale, and it seemed to Clare that it must be thankful for its five minutes of freedom each week. After washing the skin, Clare rinsed it, dried it, and then rubbed it with an alcohol swab, which made the skin tingle and removed any adhesive still clinging.

In the center of this cleansed square squirmed Clare's stoma, the bit of small intestine allowed a peek at the outside world. Guts-red and about as big around as a bottlecap, the stoma, that permanent wound, was what Clare had received in return for giving up her dying colon. Blind and writhing, a stoma could weep blood if not cared for. Clare's stoma rarely wept.

She sprinkled a protective layer of powder around the stoma, fitted the wafer over it (careful not to pinch), tamped the adhesive edges of the wafer to her stomach, then snapped the new plastic bag onto it.

After putting her bathrobe on, Clare threw out the trash, put away her supplies, and lay back down on the bed to take the nap she had never been able to have in the hospital.

Hank limped toward town, his calf burning. And as he hitched forward, the calf griping on that fine line between twinging and seizing, Hank shuddered and felt the coils of Hunt's Station tighten. Here he was, barely back after fifteen years as a ghost, and he'd inherited a dead man's room and a dead man's manuscript, ticked off Dirty Willy, snubbed Sanborn Hunt, and made love to Maggie Parriss.

He smiled at that last thought, though the smile crumbled as he remembered the night before last. He realized he had only smiled at the idea of Saturday night, at the fantasy of taking Maggie Parriss. There had been no kindness in their lovemaking, nor laughter, just fire and granite, the sharpening of knives. Maggie Parriss needed to flee Hunt's Station, while Hank Rodgers needed to ground himself in it. Maggie sought a ladder, Hank an anchor.

Hank didn't believe they were finished with one another, but he wasn't smiling anymore either.

The wind was Clare Hunt's one true companion, one of the languages she understood. Gale and gust, draft and blast, squall and zephyr, she listened to them all, smelled them, tasted them; wind whisked through her veins. She sometimes thought of her songs, all Hunt's Station songs, as just another of the wind's voices. And all that day, she had been buffeted by the wind blowing from Maggie Parriss.

Maggie and her song had taken Clare by surprise, like a sudden blizzard—or an old lover coming back to town. She hadn't been prepared for Maggie's pain and Maggie's fire. It was a song Clare wished she had written.

"I am the last child," Clare sang. "The last child."

The song had soughed through her napping dreams, and now she couldn't get rid of it, a dripping midnight faucet that can't be fixed.

"The last child. The last child. The last child."

The song drove Clare from her bed and up to the widow's walk, where the wind blew harder and where the color of the sky turned from ash to charcoal; it seemed to her that she could pluck down that sky and wrap it about her shoulders like a mourner's thick, gray shawl. Thrusting herself into the wind, Clare leaned hard against the wooden rail, trusting its strength, and stared down into town. Wind finger-combed her hair.

"I am the last child."

She smelled the rain—all loamy and wormy—before she saw it, and saw it before she felt it. The rain let go from the North, stitching the dust of Main Street one second, stinging her cheeks the next.

At the far end of Main Street she saw, as if through a screen door at dusk, somebody limping into town.

In the cold needle rain Hank shivered when he stopped to please his calf. Shirt already rain-stuck to his back, he saw no need to take cover; instead, let the rain part his hair, swamp his shoes, and streak his face. If someone had looked out the window then, drawn by the promises of the pouring rain, they would have concluded that Hank Rodgers had either gone simple or was dead standing up. They couldn't have known about his balky calf; nor could they, as Hank could, see Clare Hunt standing atop the Hunt Place as if she were waiting for something . . . somebody.

By the time Hank had hobbled up Main Street, slipped up the rain-slick lawn, and stumped up the red-brick steps, the front door to the Hunt Place was open. Hank wasn't sure whether he shuddered at that threshold because of the cold rain or because he was afraid.

He stepped inside and closed the door. He remembered the Hunt Place as a house of constant dusk, a place to wait for the end of the world. It smelled of varnish and decaying books and ancient dust and, too, of rain and wind and fresh bread. The only sounds were the thunk-thunk of the Regulator clock from the front room and the drip of water off his body.

Hank half-expected to hear kitchen clatter, Clare and her mother whispering and giggling, the rattle and chatter of domesticity. Becky Hunt had been a sliver of sunlight in this house of shadows, and, like Hank's mother, she had died young. Hunt's Station sometimes seemed to be a town defined by those who had died too soon and those who had lived too long. All Hank knew was that Becky Hunt was worth all the Sanborn Hunts there had ever been or ever would be.

Clare drifted down the stairs, light as first snow; her robe glowed wedding white in the gloom. She stood stock-still at the bottom of the stairs, staring hard at him, staring as if she might never see him again.

"It's you," she said.

He was surprised she'd spoken first. It was his obligation; he was the one who had all the explaining to do.

"Yes," he said.

Her midnight hair, her eyes quarry deep and quarry dark, her razor cheekbones, all those things overwhelmed Hank Rodgers, and he trembled. It seemed that Clare was a judgment on him. He'd weaseled away; she hadn't. The girl he'd known had vanished, and in her place waited this formidable woman. Hank knew he hadn't kept up.

"You're cold and wet," she said.

She disappeared into the dark heart of the house—Hank didn't budge—and returned with a towel, SH monogrammed on it in gold thread.

As he stood there shivering, she undressed him to his undershorts, the way you undress a little kid who's gotten soaked playing in the snow, and then dried him—rough and thorough.

"Now we can talk," Clare said.

She led him to the front-room couch, where they sat without touching. Rain drummed on the roof, wind scolded the windows, lightning scalded the sky.

"This is my weather," Clare said, "wet and gray and windy. Its bleakness echoes and aches in my bones. And when I sing, I'm the sound of the pouring rain . . . and so is, I think, Maggie Parriss." She snared Hank's eyes, set them free. "The pouring rain matters in this parched hell, Hank, and the harder it rains, the better. The water in the ground has been stolen from us, but we can still trust the water from the sky, can fill the rain barrels. And when it rains, Fire Town is quenched, at least for a while. And when it rains, we can all pretend to cry, let the rain stream down our faces like tears, because this goddamned town has even taken that away, Hank. Has even dried up our rivers of grief."

"I couldn't stay," Hank said. "I had to get out."

"And I couldn't leave."

"Clare . . ."

"I am the last child," she sang in her November voice. "The last child, the last child."

He shivered in the cold autumn of her song, his tears burning acid. He slid toward her and held her as she hummed Maggie Parriss's song, his arms and her shoulders as stiff as two-by-fours.

"You want to know what this town has done to me, Hank Rodgers? You really want to know?"

Hank said nothing.

She opened her robe. The scar, a barbwire fence of dead flesh, started just below her breasts. She gripped his hand, put his index finger at the top of the scar, then guided the finger slowly down as the scar cut across the contours of her stomach.

His fingers bumping along the scored tissue, Hank thought of ghost rails hidden deep in the dark woods.

Clare stopped his hand right above where the scar burrowed into her pubic hair and held it there, her grip strong as any man's.

"Don't you ever touch that girl again, Hank," she said, her breath blowing hot on his cheek.

He tangled his fingers in dark, curly hair, tried his hand against her strength.

"Promise me," she said.

He combed his fingers through her pubic thatch. And where he thought she might be dry . . . she was wet; he slipped his fingers inside her; she sucked in her breath.

"Promise me," she said, finally letting go.

Part Two

Part Two

7

It's Mighty Dark for Me to Travel

"Stole my beer. Those sons-ta-bitches stole my beer."

Dirty Willy melting on a milk crate outside his shack, drinking—well, more than drinking, really, more akin to swilling, knocking back WillyBrews like water. Out back of his head throbbed a lump the size of a baseball. His ribs bitched at every breath. And old Sanborn had threatened to fire him, to run him out of town over trying to take a pickaxe to Joe Bleak.

"But the sons-ta-bitches stole my beer."

A nervous black pool, Willy settled into the coming night. Once it was dark, wasn't a body in Hunt's Station could find Dirty Willy Menard if he didn't want to be found. That was why Sanborn Hunt had made him lead driver. A man who toils at toxic waste has to vanish into the seams, shake hands with the shadows . . . if not the devil.

Willy scuffled to the road, hound-snuffled the air, drained his beer and whung the empty at his shack, where it clanged but didn't break. Oh, that shack of Willy's was something.

Form taking its cue from some kind of twisted Hunt's Station function.

Willy'd built it out of empty fifty-five-gallon steel drums. After his old shack had burned—Willy shut up on how that happened—he swore he was going to build a place was fireproof. So he took his welding torch and fused together enough steel drums to make one dirt-floored room. The windows were circles—steel drums cut in half, open at both ends—with heavy-duty plastic lashed to the outside; the light limping through those bleary windows always made the inside of Willy's shack seem underwater. The place echoed cold come winter, haunted hot come summer, but Willy claimed he liked it like that.

On still summer nights, if you listened hard and the wind whispered just so, you could hear the song of Dirty Willy's shack as the drums expanded and contracted. Willy said he didn't mind the noise and that, in fact, his shack's lullaby of steel put him to sleep.

Willy lit into another beer and hit the road into the night woods . . . gripping the seams . . . dancing the shadows.

"You sons-ta-bitches stole my beer," he muttered. "And Joe Bleak made ya do it."

Lloyd Rodgers hunched to his backsteps, sucking down a Lucky Strike as the smoke from Fire Town swirled round him. Felt like he didn't know where his own smoke left off and Fire Town's started, and vice-versa. He coughed, coughed again, felt a ripple in the swamp in his chest. Sometimes it seemed to him that all that kept him alive was beer, cigarettes, and his music—especially the music; maybe, to be honest, only the music. His songs and all the songs he'd grown up on sustained him. From the moment he woke each morning till he gave in to sleep, the music flowed through his days, at times the barest trickle, at others a mighty river. Some nights the music even lapped at the shore of his dreams. A fine thing to be consumed by, he had decided.

A geyser of flame spired up through the ground some hundred yards away. Lloyd shivered. He'd never seen the flames *that* close before. He looked at his house, wondered which was going to last longer, him or the house. Fire again shot from the earth, again a hundred yards away.

White-gray ash, warm as fresh pie, floated from the sky, the always starless sky. Lloyd, his fingers still raw and stiff from Saturday night and Sunday morning, picked at the banjo, sang:

> Sugar snow, sugar snow,
> when the winds of March
> blow warm and wet.
> That's when you're bound to get
> sugar snow, sugar snow.

Lloyd smiled. Verse wasn't bad for a first try. Lots of playing to go on it yet, but there was a vein there worth working. Funny with the songs, he thought. Some of them only took five, ten minutes to write—roaring through like some big old express freight—and you never had to touch them again, just sing them the way you found them. But others would go mule on you, never quite get to where they needed to go. He had a couple songs he'd been working on for more than twenty years—songs smooth as river stones in places, but mostly stubborn and ragged and unpredictable. He liked those songs best. They tried his art and his artfulness, kept him humble, and the smallest victory satisfied him. And that's all he asked for, really, the occasional smile, some small solace from the music. He'd screwed up like any man. But in his music, at least, Lloyd Rodgers moved toward a kind of contrition and redemption. It wasn't the Grand Ole Opry and Bill Monroe and the Blue Grass Boys. But maybe it was better, just him and God and the music and small-town Saturday nights.

Lloyd coughed and flicked his Lucky into the smoky dark.

Dirty Willy shrugged his fat self up Raven's Roost, barking his gut, a drunken slug inching forward from memory in the dark; no one ever looked for anything human up Raven's Roost. The crows and the ravens studied Willy as he climbed, and he nodded at them as he passed. He didn't try talking to them, though some in Hunt's Station claimed that they could. Willy thought they were full of shit, and even if it were possible, why bother with the goddamned crows? Hard enough just talking to people. He didn't seek out the crows and ravens for their gossip, anyway. He just liked their company, their fathomless black eyes that seemed to take in all of Hunt's Station, their sideways looks, the sleek, slick, blue-black feathers. Climbing Raven's Roost felt like going to church to Dirty Willy, and the crows and the ravens were its deacons, strangely silent deacons.

Scratched up and sweat-soaked, Willy topped Raven's Roost, stretched out on a limb, and waited. He wished that he'd brought a beer, but he'd never been sure whether the crows would approve of his drinking in their tree. He closed his eyes and shivered as the breeze dried his sweat. He fell asleep humming "Old Crow Can't Jump."

As if he'd been waiting for him to fall prey to sleep, the raven dropped from a night sky the color of his wings and lighted next to Dirty Willy. But not just any raven, *the* raven, the great-grandfather raven, the boss man of the woods. King Crow some old-timers called him; even had his own Lloyd Rodgers song. He carried the wingspan of an angel and the voice of a devil. His blind eye glistened white as the full moon; his good eye gloomed as black and deep as Sanborn Hunt's lagoon.

He stared at Dirty Willy, hopped closer; this one had been climbing King Crow's tree since boyhood. He walked on Willy's chest, poised his beak right above the sleeping man's eyes, then pinched his cheek—"Ouch!"—and Willy almost fell out the tree.

Willy imagined that the raven was laughing at him but could read nothing in the bird's face; cheek blood trickled.

"I brung ya a present," said Willy, tugging two squirrel carcasses out of his coat pockets. "Roadkill. I know ya can't get no fresh meat in Hunt's Station no more."

Willy laid the squirrels out on a branch, and it seemed to him that King Crow almost purred.

"Sometimes, King Crow, I feel like you're the only friend I got."

Willy eased his blunt hand toward the bird's head. King Crow bit his fingers.

"Hey!"

And Dirty Willy knew he'd been dismissed.

Back on the ground, Willy listened to Raven's Roost rustle to life as the birds sloughed sleep from their feathers and hurried to the treetop and squirrel carrion. Willy peered up through the branches and could just make out a great cawing funnel of crows and ravens circling . . . circling . . . circling.

"Know what I miss?" Lloyd Rodgers said. "Want to know what I miss most?"

"What's that, Lloyd?" said Styles Plectrum.

"The animals," Lloyd said. "Used to be, you'd take a walk and you might see a deer or a fox or even a copperhead. All you see nowadays is those goddamned crows, and I ain't talking about Gib and his boys."

"Uh-huh," Styles said.

"Those were one of the things we used to talk about, you know. Part of everyday conversation. And it got took away from us."

Hank Rodgers shoveled a red checker forward and Styles executed a quadruple jump—chunk-chunk-chunk-chunk—to win his twenty-third game of the night, against not even a threat of a loss.

"Aw, shit," Hank said. "Good thing we ain't playing for money."

"What stupid bastard went ahead and said that?" said Styles, grinning.

"Hey, you guys want to watch your goddamned mouths out there?" Marian hollered from the kitchen. "There was ladies and children in this town once."

They all laughed, even Lloyd.

"Where's ya buddy tonight?" Lloyd asked Styles. "Ain't like Joe Bleak to miss out on your checker game."

"He ain't feeling too good," Styles said. "Decided to rest up at home tonight."

"So you got desperate and asked this one to play, huh?"

said Lloyd, pointing at Hank. "Must hardly feel like you're playing."

Styles laughed. "Oh, he's a good boy, Lloyd. You know that. You want to play a game?"

"Naw. When you guys was learning your checkers I was learning to pick my banjo."

"Hey, Lloyd," Marian called. "Play us a couple songs. I know without looking that you got that old g.d. banjo with you."

"Well, all right," Lloyd said. "That'd be fine."

Lloyd loosened his fingers, tuned the banjo. Least a man could do was play for his friends.

There's not a sane body in Hunt's Station you'd find at The Crossroads after midnight.

It was at The Crossroads, some say, that Sanborn Hunt cut the deal that damned Hunt's Station. At The Crossroads where Dirty Willy became something less than human. At The Crossroads that Hunt's Station stopped being a town and became a nightmare.

So, there's nobody you'd find at The Crossroads after midnight . . . except maybe Lloyd Rodgers . . . except maybe Dirty Willy Menard.

"What the fuck're you doing here?" Lloyd asked Willy.

"Free country, last I looked," Willy said.

"Freer for some than others, you fat little prick."

"So, Mr. Lloyd High-and-Mighty-and-Lonesome Rodgers wanted to come down The Crossroads and pick his banjo and I interrupted."

"Makes better sense than beatin' off in the dirt."

"You don't know nothing."

"Just know what Joe Bleak tells me, Willy."

"Fuck Joe Bleak."

"You're just lucky I didn't write that song, Willy boy. I wrote that song, you'd be fuckin' dead."

"What the hell're you talkin' about."

"You can kill a man with a good song, Willy. You ought to know that. Pierce him right through the fuckin' heart and make him bleed to death."

"You're crazy."

"And no man, Dirty Willy Menard, would ever take a pickaxe to me and live to tell about it. No man."

But Dirty Willy Menard had slipped into the night before Lloyd Rodgers realized that he was just talking to himself.

From midnight till daybreak, WHWM played just one song . . . over and over and over . . . "It's Mighty Dark for Me to Travel" . . . the hard-driving mandolin and banjo pursuing Hunt's Stationers through their sleepless night, Bill Monroe's lonesome Kentucky keening haunting the town till Dirty Willy slunk back to the radio station, smelling of gasoline, sulphur, and greasy rags, and changed the song.

Though he scorned them, Lloyd Rodgers couldn't keep away from Sanborn Hunt's lagoons. He was drawn to them the way other people are to car crashes or fires. Not the man-made mess that festered up the shop, but the dozens of others that oozed in the backwoods. Ponds and springs, sloughs and fishing holes, swamps and ditches that Sanborn Hunt had had the arrogance to first foul and then kill. Water that had rippled in complaint at those first steel drums but that now wept, thick and mute.

Lloyd squatted on the bank of what had once been Plectrum Pond. He'd fished that pond, swum it, skated it—even made love in it. It had been a strong strand in the skein of days that led from his boyhood to his manhood. But the pond had succumbed to the past tense, had become an old friend to mourn. All that was left now was a black hollow, as if an eye had been gouged out. And Lloyd imagined all these blind eyes, all over Hunt's Station, blank and unblinking, looking toward heaven, praying, beseeching, with no hope of ever getting their sight back. No more moonlight turning water to milk. No more stars staring at their reflections in the god-sent mirror of a calm pond.

Wherever there had been water, Sanborn Hunt had dumped. And they hadn't said a word—not one fucking word. They had been as mute as the betrayed water. Maybe they'd all been too busy—with their new pickup trucks and new shotguns and additions to their houses—to see what was happening to their town, to realize that Sanborn Hunt had bought their indifference. Lloyd shook his head, lit a cigarette, shut his eyes. He sucked the smoke hard into his lungs, and he could see the poison snakes of black liquid racing through Hunt's Station's veins. Subterranean lakes, streams, and rivers damned just as surely as Plectrum Pond. On some days, the leaching into the soil of only one drop at a time, one drop at a time. On others, thousands of gallons gurgling and gushing. And Hunt's Station rotting, rotting and dying.

But where had they been when all this happened, Lloyd asked himself. Where the hell had they been? He spit his cigarette butt into the pond—didn't even sizzle—and started to pick like he meant to bust the strings:

Mama, can you take me back to old Hunt's Station?
Down by the Cheney Mill where the golden fish played.
I'm sorry, my son, there's no use in askin'.
Mister Sanborn's crow trucks done called it away.

This is how we are forced to remember Joe Bleak:

Joe Bleak sits in the dark on his sweaty, wrinkled bed, feet flat on the floor. He shakes four aspirin from the bottle, washes them down with rye whiskey. He's been aching all over for two months now; can't make it stop. He's still wearing his work-clothes, even his workboots. He considers pulling off the boots, but the thought makes him sigh and tears rise like fish feeding at dusk, and he doesn't. His legs and arms feel heavy, hundred-pound sacks of sand. But his head hangs even heavier, like it could just snap off and roll across the floor, like a sunflower too big for its stalk. He manages another gulp of rye, shudders, and waits for the whiskey heat to warm him. He has been hiding here, on his bed, since he got home from work, flirting with tears, ratcheting his rage up and down, flinching at the past and recognizing no future. He sees himself as a gray piece of wood sucked dry by time and carpenter ants, and he almost smiles. He shivers, more whiskey. He clicks on the radio— "It's Mighty Dark for Me to Travel" raves on WHWM—then grunts his legs, workboots and all, up onto the bed, where he slumps back into the pillows, panting.

"All I need's a couple days' sleep," he whispers. "Couple days' sleep."

When "It's Mighty Dark for Me to Travel" starts up on the radio for the fourth time, Joe Bleak bellows, "Someone ought to hang that fucking Dirty Willy!"

He thinks about shutting the radio, but leaning over isn't quite worth the effort right then. It's all I can do to breathe, he thinks before he passes out, 's all I can do.

Dirty Willy poured gasoline around Joe Bleak's place like an old man watering a garden, bent and scuffling, making sure to give the ground a good soaking. He splashed gasoline on Joe's front steps, and he splashed gasoline on Joe's back steps; he doused the outer walls with gasoline; and he shinnied up a tree to rain gasoline on the roof. He snugged gasoline-soaked rags around the base of the house and then circled it, sowing lit matches; he climbed the tree again to seed matches on the roof.

"Well, Joe Bleak," Dirty Willy hissed, "let's see what you find when you get home from your goddamned checker game tonight."

The fire garden blossomed just as Willy had hoped: flames sprouted at the base of the house as tendrils of fire raced and writhed up the walls; the roof bloomed yellow, red, and blue; wood cracked and crackled. Willy's cheeks prickled at the heat.

And when he tasted fresh ash, Dirty Willy Menard smiled for the first time in a long, long while.

8

A Deeper Shade of Blue

On the morning of Joe Bleak's funeral, Hank woke with the sun. He looked at Maggie Parriss—her face not yet gone to crevices and creases, her body pale and smooth—and it felt like stealing. But when she had banged at his door the night before, crying and fidgeting and gnawing at her lower lip, still just a girl, after all, he hadn't the will to refuse her. Making love with his wife made Hank feel like another person, some Hank Rodgers impersonator. Clare made him almost whole, almost the Hank Rodgers he'd once been. But Maggie Parriss was all about selfishness, greed, and possession, as if he were Sanborn Hunt and Maggie were Hunt's Station. Strong as she was, Maggie'd been there to be taken and he'd taken her, in pure, practical Hunt's Station meanness. Her youth and her strength and her hunger to leave Hunt's Station angered him, he realized, because he had lost those things and would never have them again.

As Maggie slept, Hank kneeled between her legs and licked her, knifing his tongue up and down. As she trembled from her deep sleep, he forced his way inside and pounded at her like driving a nail.

Maggie Parriss never made a sound.

Main Street drowsed quiet, like a drunk on Sunday morning. Marian's Cafe, open Christmas and Thanksgiving, was closed. On funeral days, Hunt's Stationers fasted till sundown; they knew you couldn't truly taste the brine and ashes of death on a full stomach. The bitter, burnt-wood smell of the Bleak fire still stained the air; couldn't draw a breath without remembering that Joe Bleak was dead—burned to death, the poor bastard. The crows and the ravens drifted high above, haunting the new day, but quiet, expectant, as if they too were in mourning.

Indoors, grief snuggled into beds and pulled the covers tight, settled into big overstuffed chairs that smelled of mildew, and seduced husbands and wives right in front of their spouses. Communal and private, it was a compounded grief that grew with each Hunt's Station death. Slow and consuming, it was a grief that devoured the heart.

Styles Plectrum stared out the kitchen window, chain-smoking against his hunger. He'd gotten to the fire first, not that it'd mattered. His cousin's house had been engulfed—no way in, no way out—and Styles had turned away and waited for the fire trucks. He had known Joe was in there, but he'd also known there was little point in both of them dying for the sake of some grand, suicidal heroism. No sense in giving Dirty Willy Menard double satisfaction. Not that Styles was thinking much about Dirty Willy. They all knew he did it, and they all knew he was out there, ghosting through the dark woods, giving no thought to leaving Hunt's Station; Willy Menard was just as trapped as they were, maybe even more. But today was Joe Bleak's day, and Styles'd be damned if he was going to let Dirty Willy spoil that.

Lloyd Rodgers contemplated an old gift, a custom-made banjo: handcrafted, walnut neck, staghorns inlaid in abalone, gold-plated hardware, satin finish. But now one side of it was caved in and bloodstained, three strings snapped, the neck twisted and cracked. One year, when there had been so much money in town that people hadn't known what to spend it on, Sanborn Hunt had given the banjo to Lloyd as a bonus. But Lloyd had hardly ever picked it up, had never played it. He had stuck with the ancient banjo that'd been his grandfather's. Lloyd had accepted Sanborn Hunt's gift, admired its heft, brought it home, shoved it under the bed, and almost forgotten about it. How could a man play true music, the blood music, on an instrument that Sanborn Hunt had touched? Lloyd lit a cigarette, kept staring at the banjo.

Clare Hunt put on a plain black dress, pulled her hair back hard from her forehead, and sat barefoot on her front steps.

The funeral procession began at the Hunt Waste Management end of Main Street, where all of the town's funeral processions started, as if the mere knowledge of HWM at their backs put everyone into the right frame of mind for a funeral. Styles and Lloyd were the lead pallbearers of the six gray men chosen to carry Joe Bleak's plain pine burying box. But even more than by the pallbearers, Joe Bleak was borne to his early grave by the weeping and wailing fiddles hidden along the way.

Dozens of silent Hunt's Stationers, comfortable in their grays and blacks, walked behind Joe Bleak to The Crossroads, where he'd often said he wanted to be buried. "At The Cross-roads," Joe had said, "I figure a man has an even shot at heaven or hell, and I'm not sure what kind of mood I'm going to be in."

There wasn't the usual funeral chatter and gossip, that crow-talk people discover at someone's death. Joe Bleak had died before his time, reminding all of them that they probably would too, and none of them had found the words for it yet; the fiddles would have to do as they had for so long.

As the procession snaked left in front of the Hunt Place, Clare stood. Each year the coffins seemed to get heavier, the backs more bent, the processions shorter. Some year soon, she imagined, there would be no one strong enough left to bear and bury the dead; shacks and houses would simply be boarded up, the corpses still inside, the crows and the ravens complaining on the rooves.

There were no holy men left in Hunt's Station. All the priests and reverends and preachers had finally blanched in the face of the town's overwhelming sin and fled, leaving Hunt's Stationers to grapple with God and the mysteries on their own. And, to be honest, the townspeople liked it that way.

So when the pallbearers, sweat-soaked, dust-coated, and arm-weary, set the coffin down smack in the middle of The Crossroads, it was Styles Plectrum, not some God-drunk stranger, who said the last words over Joe Bleak.

As the crowd settled, Styles leaned against the closed casket—there was no gawking at the dead in Hunt's Station. After some minutes, Styles stood up straight and cleared his throat:

"Like all of us, Joe Bleak traveled miles and miles and

miles of loneliness. And, like all of us, he was just trying not to fall."

Marian's sobs caught them by surprise. In Hunt's Station, tears were a thing as rare as an eclipse or a rainbow. The men stiffened, rusted in place at the sight of Marian quaking, the tears trickling down her cheeks. But the women, their emotions oiled by her tears, rushed to her, surrounded her in a living womb. Styles gave his head a quick shake; he hadn't realized that Joe and Marian were lovers.

"Joe was the kind of man," Styles continued, "who would rather be alone on a blustery ridge than overshadowed in the comfort of a valley."

Lloyd Rodgers clenched his fists and nodded hard.

"We were like brothers, me and Joe Bleak. When we was kids, it seemed to us that we had four parents looking after each of us, not just two. We played cowboys and Indians together, and he always let me be John Wayne. We hunted and fished together. Raced our cars on The Whispering Turnpike together. And we always stuck up for each other. You could never pick a fight with just Joe Bleak or Styles Plectrum. It was always a two-for-one deal. But today there's no more together."

Hank Rodgers and Maggie Parriss caught each other's eye. Hank turned away first.

"You know, they say it was the smoke that killed my cousin, not the flames. But I guess none of us should be surprised by that. Most of us learn young to watch out for the flames; but no one learns us about the smoke. And we've been sucking down Sanborn Hunt's smoke for years."

Sanborn Hunt stood at the shadow edge of the crowd, almost in the trees. He wore a too-tight black suit shiny with age. He hadn't arrived with the procession, and most of the townspeople hadn't noticed him; a few looked back, whispered, pointed. His face, emotionless and granite-hard, never changed, not even when King Crow flapped from the trees and lighted on his shoulder.

"Because even though we're here to honor Joe Bleak, I just can't get Sanborn Hunt out of my mind. He killed our town. He killed our mothers and fathers, our husbands and wives, our sons and daughters. He killed Joe Bleak, and he's still killing us.

"That Keegan kid too. Sanborn Hunt certainly killed him. I think about that kid every day, his head stove in, floating in that goddamned lagoon. Let's lay him at Sanborn's doorstep too."

Sanborn and Styles locked eyes, Sanborn neither moved nor unmoved. Styles, scouring the murderer's face, found nothing, neither guilt nor freedom from guilt. He may as well have been peering into the bottom of a dead, snake-infested well as into a man's eyes.

The sun, one of those dull, angry summer suns, bore down. The modest breeze that'd been teasing shriveled and died.

Styles dry-swallowed, licked his cracked lips.

"Boy, we all thought we was something once upon a time, didn't we? Just thought we was the nuts. All we had to do was look the other way, and ol' Sanborn'd slide that green into our greedy paws.

"But you want to know what makes us really mad? What really ticks us off? It's that we know we deserve every goddamned bad thing that's happened to us ever since. And that we're guilty, that we're just as low as Sanborn Hunt.

"We're Sanborn Hunt's accomplices.

"Dirty Willy Menard works for all of us.

"We all killed Joe Bleak."

Styles heeled away from his friends and his enemies, gave his broad back to the townspeople, and traced the dust tracks on Joe Bleak's coffin like he was a fortuneteller slinking up and down the lifelines of a rich widow's palm. And when he spoke again, he didn't turn around.

"Sometimes Joe, you know he'd say to me, 'Styles, we ought to just burn this fucking town down and start over again somewhere else. Because we ain't never getting it back. We give it all away.'

"Now you tell me he wasn't right. Just try to fucking tell me he ain't right."

They all scuffled back to town even more quiet than they had come. And when the last of them had gone, Styles stripped to the waist and started to dig; he'd refused help from Lloyd Rodgers and everyone else.

He would spade Joe Bleak's grave alone. He would lower Joe Bleak's burying box alone. And he would cover Joe Bleak's grave alone. It was his job—his alone.

But when Styles Plectrum had bitten only two foot deep, he struck black water, that rot pumped from the heart of his town. Thick and dark as Sanborn Hunt's eyes, it coiled from the wounded earth and pooled like dusk at Styles's feet.

That afternoon, Hunt's Station ceased.

As the paint-blistering, bone-bleaching sun snarled and gnawed at Hunt's Station, the town stopped being a town. It stopped breathing, and there was no one there to give it mouth-to-mouth. It shuddered as decades-old bonds, some of them centuries old, groaned and frayed.

The people flinched at the idea of community, shook their heads at the notion of a common good, severed all ties, and hid.

Main Street, stark and empty, was left to the mercy of the punishing sun.

Bare-chested men disappeared into dark, suffocating attics with sweating six-packs of beer.

Women huddled in cool dirt cellars, clutching their fiddles.

They first sought the secret places of the body, then sought the secret places of the heart. A doomed people, blamed and blaming, seeking the womb, pining to be once again, separate and selfish, immersed in absolute innocence. Retreating inside as far as they dared go, straddling that fault line where guilt and depression grapple.

Styles Plectrum had pulled the thread, and they had unraveled.

Come late afternoon, a fortress of gray and black clouds, crowned by barbwire lightning, bulked to the North. The humid air hung udder heavy. And the leaves riffled, showing their pale fishbellies. But no rain. Thunder grumbled and stumbled and rumbled as the sky came black and low. But again, no rain. Lightning spit and sizzled. Still no rain. The wind flung the gravel of Main Street first north and then south and then north again. No rain. Ragged whips of lightning cracked above the town, thunder freight-trained through, wind ripped gates from their hinges.

No rain.

On some days, you couldn't even get the sky above Hunt's Station to cry.

Out at The Crossroads, Styles squatted atop Joe Bleak's coffin, watching the black water ooze from the half-dozen or so holes where he'd meant to bury his cousin. Squatted there like if he stayed long enough, a solution to his problem would come walking down the road complete with a fifty-year guarantee.

"Shit," Styles Plectrum said. "Shit, shit, shit, shit."

He sighed and slithered off the coffin. The Crossroads had gotten muddy with the black water, and Styles's shoes squished as he walked.

So gripped had Styles been in trying to bury his cousin, he hadn't noticed the day gravy up on him, had heard but hadn't really heard all that racketing thunder and lightning, hadn't felt the charged air almost crackle, or seen the faint bristling of the hair on his arms. So deep had Styles gone that he'd forgotten that only a fool dared The Crossroads during a thunderstorm.

He snatched up his shovel, but the next thing Styles Plectrum knew, there was a flash, a snick, and a snap, and he was face-first in the black water—momentarily deaf, blind, and drowning in mud.

There was heat at his back—Joe Bleak's coffin burning.

Blinking, his ears still ringing, Styles just wallowed there in the black mud as the fire swarmed the coffin.

Now there's a man, Styles Plectrum thought, who was meant to burn.

And then he laughed, great deep belly laughs that threw

him back into the muck and kept on until his stomach ached and ached again.

And still, it didn't rain.

In the utter dark, long past sundown and dusk, the men, hungry and still thirsty, wobbled down from their attics. The women, hungry too, crept up from their cellars, still fiddle-clinging. The lights eased on in Marian's Cafe and in Tater Tate's Tavern, reassuring Main Street. Silent, afraid to look at each other—fearing more what they might give away than what they might see—the men and women bathed and showered and washed up. When they did look at each other, they saw only the night ahead, heard distant music. Each one embraced the night alone, and no one made any promises of return.

Tater Tate laid out his usual free funeral-day spread: hummocks of potato and macaroni salad, barrels of Granite State potato chips, and platter upon platter of ham, turkey, salami, Swiss, and provolone. And the beer—always plenty of beer—was WillyBrew, of course. In one corner of the bar, Gib Crow and his sons, Those G.D. Crows, were setting up to play.

Anchored to the bar, a splintery slab of oak as strong and substantial as Tate himself, Tater watched his friends escape into his hospitality. It pleased him to see shoulders unknot and hands blossom as the men ducked inside; he believed that his tavern was the last place in Hunt's Station where a man could relax, be himself. Outside his doors, the millstones of guilt and memory waited to grind a man into bonemeal. But tonight . . . tonight, Tater Tate will fill your hollow gut, get you skunk-humping drunk, and make sure the band plays the old songs. You might never want to leave.

Gib Crow thunked at the microphone with his forefinger and then cackled into it.

"This here song was one of Joe Bleak's favorites. It's one I wrote about Tater's bar . . . 'Sawdust and Shadows.' "

> Well, sawdust and shadows,
> that's all they sell here.
> Just sawdust and shadows,
> chased with a beer.
> But sawdust and shadows,
> you're now my home.
> 'Cause sawdust and shadows,
> I'm too tired to roam.

When Gib and his boys finished, the men dropped their sandwiches and clapped, booming their big, rough working-man's mitts. They hooted and choked on their beer. They clapped some more and knocked over their beers. Tater was already spreading more sawdust on the floor.

"Play it again, Gib! Come on!"

"We love that damn song, Gib!"

"For Joe, Gib! Pick it for Joe!"

And Those G.D. Crows played "Sawdust and Shadows" again, and not for the last time that night.

"Them guys sure pick it," Hank said to Howie Brown. "I'd forgotten how good they are."

"You ought to know," Howie said, "what with your old man and all."

Hank nodded, his forehead already prickling with the beer.

"Y'old man coming out tonight?" Howie asked. "We don't see him much no more."

Hank shrugged.

"No figuring him."

Howie inhaled half his beer.

"You know, everybody talks about how fuckin' good your old man is on that banjo of his, but I'll tell ya, Hank, he was one hell of a stock-car driver too. One wall-bangin' cot-sucker. When the bunch of us use to race over to The Pines—you remember that old racetrack in Miles' Grant?—he ran this milk-white '37 Pontiac coupe with a banjo painted on it. I'll tell ya, that little mother could go."

Al Crockett, three beers snug in each bear paw, stumbled into their table and thumped into a chair, WillyBrew sloshing onto the already sticky, beer-slick Formica.

"Hey, Al," Howie said, "you remember that little Ponny Lloyd Rodgers used to run at The Pines? Sweet, white number?"

"Shit, yes," Al said. "Put me into the puckerbrush any number of times. Course, I had old Lloyd chewing on the trees a few times myself."

Howie and Al shook their heads as slow, smooth, and liquid as ale and memory, each draining his frosted mug.

"He give up the racing after he married my mother," Hank said. "I never got to see him. Kept that Pontiac running, though. Stored it out to the shed."

"Oh, we all kept our cars," Howie said. "Even after they shut down The Pines."

"I remember you guys used to race out on The Whispering Turnpike when I was a kid," Hank said. "You do that anymore?"

Howie and Al glanced at each other, hid in their beers.

"What's the matter?"

"The Whispering Turnpike," Howie said, "that's serious business nowadays."

"Road just keeps getting stronger every year," Al said. "Whispers harder and harder and harder."

"You don't run The Whisperin' no more, unless you mean it," Howie said. "Not unless you fuckin' mean it."

"We lost two a the Mountain boys out there last year," Al said. "And Billy Murphy lost an eye, got himself laid up six months."

The men lapsed into silence, let the beer and bluegrass music break over them. Al wandered off for more beer.

"Hank," Howie said.

"Huh? What?" Hank said.

"Don't talk about The Whispering too much."

Hank stared into Howie's hatchet face.

"We think about it all the time—the roar of the engine in your balls . . . the pounding in your ears . . . a road so straight and quick. Next time I drive The Whispering Turnpike, I ain't coming back."

Up on Jerusalem Ridge, up at The Chimneys, the women fiddle.

They fiddle together, they fiddle in ones and twos, they fiddle the way they have for hundreds of years: they fiddle for Joe Bleak and all the others taken leave too soon . . . fiddle for their men, raging, lost and worn out . . . for themselves, each note a stitch meant to mend the rent fabric of community. Freight-train fast they fiddle, stoking that Gloryland Express, and freight-train slow, the train haunting, slate and white, through their hearts on a blizzard day. Sweet and sour they play, soft and hard, weaving a womb of music about The Chimneys.

They sip at their cold summer soups—brambleberry and blueberry and rhubarb—and gnaw on salads ripped fresh from their gardens, and on dark, thick-crusted breads that taste of fate, loam, and tears.

Iris and Alison Rodgers huddle, their heads just touching in a sisterly fiddling conspiracy . . . Maggie Parriss, knees flush to her chest, sits and rocks, eyes closed, imagining an endless night in which she is the only fiddler up on Jerusalem Ridge, the only woman left in town . . . and ancient Irene Taylor, the town elder, embraces one of the chimneys, mottled cheek pressed to the stones; she sops up what's left of the day's heat and listens, listens for the old music, the primeval tones that only those stones would know.

On they play, eyes shut and hearts open, their music honeying into the stolen-star night . . . an offering, their sole hedge against oblivion. The old ladies, in their blue-veined, wasp-paper skin, creak up now and, their hands all bone and gristle and knuckle, clasp each other and turn in lazy Ferris wheel circles, their gray and brown dresses belling and flaring. The ebb and flow of hem, the cotton nuzzling ankles, conjure vanished Saturday nights when their legs were hard and strong, their breasts sweet and tender, when they first learned to flirt, to chase, to be chased. They would never again be so powerful.

These women, still strong enough to look within, that is to say, still look toward heaven—and hell—and not flinch, their hearts bleakened, their souls aching . . . they can still draw heaven near with their fiddling and dancing, winch heaven to the very tops of The Chimneys.

So, they saw their bows, carpenters building a cathedral of music toward heaven because, somehow, as the hard times grow, God beckons even more furiously . . . but so, too, does some ancient voice in the fieldstones, a voice from God, or from before the idea of God . . . something touched by creation and the billion billion cooling years.

And there, in the shadow of a shadow of the oldest chimney, Maggie Parriss trembles and sobs into the knobby arms of her great-aunt, Irene Taylor, who strokes her forehead and shushes, "There, there, dear. There, there."

Lloyd Rodgers leaned hard on the fender of Dirty Willy's pickup. He clutched the battered, beaten, and bloodstained banjo that Sanborn Hunt had once given him. He closed his eyes, heard the women fiddling up to Jerusalem Ridge, and shrugged his shoulders like a boxer about to enter the ring. He picked at the banjo's two good strings, then walked around back to the truck bed, gravel crackling under his workboots. Dirty Willy's house of steel griped and groaned, and Lloyd almost jumped. Two crows scrackled in the trees. He eased the banjo into the truckbed, covered it with a blanket. He stopped and looked back twice before he got to the road. Standing with his back to Willy's place, he listened again to the fiddlers and wished he were playing with them. As much as he tried to cloak the night about him and leave Willy's, he couldn't.

His mouth worked, but no words came out. He sighed and crunched back to the truck, kicking the fender a good one as he passed. He threw back the blanket, plucked the banjo out, and scuffed home.

———

Men slept on porches and men slept in alleys. Some men even slept curled in the gravel of Main Street, twitching like dogs.

Hank and Howie Brown sat quiet on the steps to Marian's, Howie smoking and Hank nursing one last beer. Howie pulled hard on his cigarette and Hank could hear the tobacco crackle as it burned. Hank poured out the last of his beer, beer-made mud splashing his ankles, and set the empty on the step.

"Had enough, huh?" Howie said.

"Guess," Hank said.

"My old lady's gonna be somethin' pissed."

Hank shrugged, snorted a laugh.

"It don't never change," Howie said. "I ain't saying it's bad, but it don't never change."

"I never felt like I was married," Hank said. "Felt like I was pretending, playing house."

"I ain't got that problem. I'm married, all right."

"Some of us ain't fit to be married."

"Look, there's Clare Hunt."

Hank looked up Main Street to the Hunt Place, where Clare stood on the widow's walk. Even at that distance, it seemed to Hank that she was staring straight at him . . . waiting.

"Maybe she's gonna sing," Howie said.

"I'd be surprised," Hank said.

"She's a good kid. Beautiful voice."

"Yeah."

"Old man's a prick, though. Through and through."

"Makes you wonder how he ever got a daughter like her."

Howie shrugged, and when they looked up again she was gone.

The door was open, though the house was dark.

"Clare? . . . Clare?"

The refrigerator hummed, the Regulator clock thunked. Hank creaked up the stairs, his head suddenly clear. He wasn't sure what he was doing there in Clare's night house, wasn't sure he had been beckoned.

She waited at the top of the stairs, looking out the window, studying the dark woods the way some people study the Bible that time of night.

"Clare?"

She struck hard and fast, slapping his face and raking his cheek in one motion. "I'm too old for this shit," she hissed. "Do you understand? Too goddamned old."

Hank's face sizzled.

"I guess I deserved that."

"You can't come traipsing back to this town and have it both ways, Hank Rodgers. I won't let you. You owe me. You owe this town."

She tugged off her nightgown—"Leave Maggie Parriss alone"—and threw it at Hank.

"Do . . . you . . . understand . . . me?"

She pushed Hank onto the floor.

"Do you?" she asked.

"Yes."

"You better, Hank Rodgers. Because as far as you're concerned, I'm Hunt's Station . . . these are Hunt's Station . . . and this is Hunt's Station."

She lowered herself onto Hank like a woman testing a hot bath.

"There," she whispered humid into his ear. "There. Doesn't that feel like home? Doesn't that . . . feel . . . like . . . fucking . . . the earth?"

9

Mystery Train

As night coiled to her blackest hour, a train keened long and lonesome over toward Fire Town. Clare, rocking there in the bedroom dark, savoring her house of shadows and spirits, cocked her head toward the open window and listened hard —like trying to capture a dying mother's last whispers.

The train sobbed again, nearer now.

She knew that train whistle as well as the sound of her own heartbeat. Had been expecting it, really, would have been disappointed if she hadn't heard it.

"Hank," she hissed, shaking him from his humid half-sleep. "Hank, come with me."

Clare led him to the roof, to the widow's walk and the starless night; smoke from Fire Town lazed in the treetops.

"Listen," she said.

The train moaned its blues . . . grief on the rails.

"Just some train," he said, his head gauzy with sleep.

"But it's here, Hank. Here in town. *Here.*"

"So?"

"But, Hank . . . there haven't been any trains in Hunt's Station for over twenty years."

They listened to the train whine and wind through the night woods, where Hank knew no rails could possibly lie. But this train was no Fireball Mail, no Orange Blossom Special. This was a sorrow train . . . slow . . . patient . . . hypnotic . . . a lover taking her sweet, sweet, sweet time.

"It's the ghost train, Hank," Clare said. "That long, black mystery train come to bear Joe Bleak away. I heard it for the first time the night my mother died."

"But—"

"Sshh . . . sshh."

Hank shut his eyes and let the train, that impossible mystery train, steal through his veins . . . heard the swish of steam . . . saw only the shadow of the engineer.

Hank swore he heard a muffled cry of "All aboard!" and he opened his eyes.

"What the hell?" he said.

Clare smiled.

"What're you smiling at?"

"That train, Hank, that mystery train and its depots of despair. It only makes stops in towns like Hunt's Station . . . towns that have lost, or given away, their souls . . . the towns that have vanished from maps and memory . . . the drowned towns and burned-down towns . . . towns buried by mountain and desert . . . towns done in by whirlwind and wishes.

"It's a wonder you ever found your way back here, Hank. Truly a wonder."

Clare stood and stared down into Main Street, leaning hard against the rail, daring it to give. She sighed.

"Ain't much, is it, Hank? A few stores, a dirt road, decent

people, and all the woods you could ever want—and my old man went ahead and raped it, killed it.

"I don't even know him, Hank. Never did. Isn't even my father no more. He's some local myth. To me, he's as dead as my mother—maybe more—as dead as this town.

"But this is where we belong, ain't it? I've been out there, too, Hank. I know we ain't fit to live out there, beyond The Crossroads. We don't know how to get along. Out there, we're just the dust on a moth's wings.

"Hunt's Station is where you belong, Hank Rodgers . . . where I belong. You can only kid yourself for so long. This town might be dead, damned, and disappeared, but you're happy here, stripped to your Hunt's Station self. Your real self.

"Admit it. Admit it, Hank Rodgers."

"Sshh, Clare. Sshh."

The train wailed one more time, that last cry before a mother sees her stillborn baby lowered into the ground.

"There it goes," Clare said. "In constant mourning, like this town . . . like me . . . like all of us. Running on its own time . . . running on Lonesome Standard Time."

Hank went to Clare and held her. And as her body loosened, unknotted against his, Clare felt like home to Hank, and he could feel his parched, empty places start to fill.

"Deep calleth unto deep," Clare whispered. "Deep calleth unto deep."

10

You Don't Know My Mind

Marian, ever skeptical of sitting down, stood in the doorway of her café—cigarette loose in her right hand, black coffee in the other—glaring toward the East, daring the sun to rise.

She was up out of habit only and had no intention of opening the café. She refused to pretend it was business as usual; no one would expect her to. But there'd be no more crying, she'd decided not in public anyway. Marian wondered how many rivers of grief rolled and rilled through Hunt's Station nights.

A black truck creaked out of the daybreak woods and wobbled onto Main Street, steel drums stumbling against one another in the truckbed. The driver, Chickie LeClerc, nodded as he crept past. Marian nodded back, words too slippery that time of day.

She took a long pull on her cigarette, chasing it with the muddy coffee. Both of them, the smoke and the coffee, warm but bitter, like making love to someone you know has made up his mind to leave you. She sighed one of her all-purpose, every-care-in-the-world sighs and tossed her spent cigarette into the road.

"Now what would ol' Sanborn say, he saw you littering up his town like that?" Hank Rodgers said.

Marian looked at Hank, looked up the hill to the Hunt Place, and almost smiled. "And look what Dirty Willy's drugged in," she said.

Hank laughed, but the morning silence gobbled it up quick and he quieted.

"How are you, Marian?"

She shrugged, smiled a crooked smile.

"Same as always . . . only more so."

Hank peered into her composed granite face—searching, prying, seeking a handhold. But Marian's was a face to blunt all tools.

"Whatever it is you're looking for, it ain't there, Hank."

His turn to shrug, to look away.

A dog limped out of the alley next to Ken Meyer's Hardware. He didn't have a left hind leg. Dirty Willy'd hit him once with an HWM truck—hadn't even stopped, not that anyone'd been surprised.

The dog—called On'y because "He on'y has three legs" —fetched a patch of early sun and melted into it as if he needed to thaw his blood.

"Seems every town has one, don't it?" Marian said.

"What's that?" Hank said.

"Don't it seem like every small town has a three-legged dog? Some poor old bastard that got run over by a tractor or shot up or bit bad by a hog. Don't it seem like?"

"Yeah . . . I guess," Hank said.

"But it don't seem to faze him. He goes around with all

the other dogs, barking and begging and bluffing with the best of them. Mounting the lady dogs. He don't get cheated."

Hank looked at him, sitting there with his eyes closed, as if the sun were scratching his ears.

"We all should be missing a leg and be so happy," Marian said.

Hank trudged the stairs to his room, finally feeling the weight of the past day and the past night. He shucked his shirt, shook off his dungarees, and plunged into bed. He didn't notice that the lock had already been tripped, didn't see the letter slipped under the door.

When he woke, his mouth sand, his head sledgehammering, Hank knew it was past noon, and he groaned. The room had surrendered its morning vigor, become prisoner to thick afternoon heat. Out the corner of his eye he saw the plain white envelope on the floor. And though one part of him wanted to ignore the letter just then, he couldn't. He reached for it from his bed, but came up short. He stretched half out of the bed, but still couldn't grab it. Then three-quarters. Finally, his toes digging into the edge of the mattress, he dived at the letter and snagged it, a shortstop lunging deep into the hole. He also smacked his chin on the floor—"Shit!"—but he had managed not to get out of bed.

After reeling himself in, Hank opened the letter. It was from his sisters, Alison and Iris, asking him to come out to their house that night. And though he was the only son, and though he was the oldest, his sisters scared him. He'd fled and left them with the old man; he'd escaped, they hadn't. He'd gone, and in that leaving had become weaker; they'd stayed and become strong in their music and in their burden. It mattered to Hank what they thought of him, and he feared what they thought.

Hank sighed out of bed, clicked on WHWM—"Shootin' Creek" by Charlie Poole and the North Carolina Ramblers— poured a glass of tomato juice, and slouched at the empty table. He'd never liked an empty table. An empty table, with its cigarette burns, knife scars, and water stains, whispered to him of transience and loneliness. His mother had never left tables empty: Fresh flowers, lace doilies, and potted plants had been her weapons against the emptiness. Sometimes he wondered whether he hadn't married just to avoid empty tables.

And as he sat there, his mind adjusting to the empty table the way your eyes adjust to the dark, he realized Keegan's manuscript was gone.

"What?"

He glanced around the room as if the manuscript might have gotten up and settled into a more comfortable chair or stretched out on the couch.

"Damn it!"

He banged open and pounded shut the cupboards. He checked under the sink, peered under the bed, and poured out the trash. But he knew it was gone.

"Sonuvabitch!"

Hank dressed, slammed out the door, and nearly trampled Maggie Parriss on the stairs.

"Christ, watch it!" Maggie said.

"Sorry, Maggie," Hank said, "but—"

"Where're you off to in such a big hurry?"

"Maggie, I, I really got to go."

Maggie Parriss, standing two steps below Hank Rodgers,

looked up at him and then shoved him so hard he whumped down on the stairs.

"You better have a minute for me," she said. "You best better have."

"Look, Maggie."

"You're a sonuvabitch, Hank Rodgers. Ain't you, though? You're no better than the rest of them. You belong here in this goddamned town."

Hank reached to touch her shoulder—"Maggie"—she jerked back.

"Don't you touch me! Fucking you ain't getting me out of this town. Ain't nobody getting me out of this frigging place except me. Except me!"

Maggie trembled there in the hall shadows, trembled between Hank Rodgers and the future. She studied Hank's blank Hunt's Station face, a face to tell everything, but a face to give away nothing. A deep, black pool on a windless night.

"I have to go," he said.

She let him pass.

Hank found Styles Plectrum smoking a cigarette on the Town Hall steps. As strong and worn as the granite upon which he sat, Styles looked permanent, like he'd been poured there.

"Uh-oh," he said, without looking up, "here comes trouble."

"Ain't you never at your office?" Hank asked.

"What the hell I need an office for when I got the Town Hall steps?"

"I suppose."

"Ain't never heard of no one looking for me who couldn't find me. They always find me, damn it. No getting around that."

Hank sat next to Styles, who smelled of woodsmoke.

"How're you making out anyway, Styles?" he asked.

Styles spit out his cigarette—"None of your fucking business"—and ground it beneath the heel of his workboots.

Hank lapsed into silence, while Styles reclaimed his.

Hank started to say something else, but Styles turned on him.

"Just leave me alone, okay? Just get your ass out of here and leave me the fuck alone."

Hank swore he could see the fires that'd claimed Joe Bleak smoldering in Styles Plectrum's eyes. Paul Keegan's stolen manuscript would have to wait.

"Ain't been to work in more'n a week," Lloyd Rodgers said. "Don't know if I'm ever gonna go back neither. Chickie says Sanborn wants to make me foreman. Can you imagine that shit? Me, the fuckin' foreman. I'd fire all their no-good, lazy asses."

Lloyd laughed a raspy cackle that to Hank sounded more like a cough than a laugh.

"Can you imagine?" Lloyd said again. "Can you goddamn imagine?"

They both laughed, drained their WillyBrews, and cracked two more.

"They better catch that fuckin' Dirty Willy pretty soon," Lloyd said, "or we're going to goddamned run out of WillyBrew."

"How much you got left?" Hank asked.

"Two, three cases. Enough for a couple more days, anyways."

"So . . . what the hell you been doing, you ain't going to work?"

"Picking . . . drinking . . . mean-eyeing Fire Town . . . wondering when one those spits of flame's gonna come busting up through the living-room floor." He coughed . . . Willy-Brewed it away.

The two of them, Lloyd Rodgers and Hank Rodgers, guttered in Lloyd's shadow kitchen, where, for the smoke from Fire Town, you couldn't tell whether it was day or night. Barechested, more bone than skin, Lloyd drank there wearing only his baggy undershorts.

"Howie Brown and Al Crockett was telling me about how you used to race with those guys in the old days over to Miles' Grant," Hank said. "Said you were pretty good."

Lloyd almost smiled. "Yeah, we had us a time," he said. "Had us a time."

"What made you give it up?"

"Don't know, really."

"Huh?"

" 'S like anything else. Just happens. I loved to race, you know; almost as much as the music. Thought it was the balls. Loved the fire and the steel and the hot rubber, the chance I might get my skull stove in. If there hadn't a been the risk, it wouldn'ta been worth it. That's why I keep playing the music: the risk is still there.

"But, you know, you get to a certain age and you think you got to give up some the things you love. Think you got to get totally serious. But that's bullshit, you know. I shoulda never quit racing, shoulda never quit playing hardball. Thank God, I never give up the music."

Lloyd sighed and opened another beer.

"Whatever happened to that race car?" Hank asked. "We used to fool around in it when we was kids."

"Oh, I still got it," Lloyd said. "Keep it running. It's out to the back shed. Key's in it, you ever want to take her out."

"Uh-huh."

They drank in silence, father and son, the beer thick and bitter. The only sounds were the hiss of bottlecaps . . . the tired gulp of tilted beer bottles . . . Lloyd's constant cough.

Hank stared at his father in drunken intensity and saw a haggard Halloween haunt, a beer-swilling skeleton whose bottomless black eyes had sunk so deep that you had to risk falling in to get a good look, whose face had been honed by rage, sorrow, and silence.

"That's it, boy," Lloyd said, "take a good, long look. Maybe it'll learn ya something." He plucked at an imaginary banjo, hummed a song his son didn't know.

Hank shook his head, and the beer made him stupid.

"It's such a fuckin' shame," he said. "You could've really been something."

"What'd you say?"

Right there, Hank knew it was all over.

"What did you say to me?" Lloyd demanded again.

"You heard."

Lloyd's chalk face blotched red and purple. His voice shook, broke, and shook some more. *"Could've* really been something?" he said.

"You know what I meant," Hank said.

"Could've been something?"

Hank refused to flinch.

"Yeah . . . *could've."*

"Well, let me tell you, Mister Man, I *was* something. I *am* something. Just because I didn't run away from this goddamn town don't mean my music, my songs, don't count. They're out there. They exist. And most of 'em are pretty damn good. Far's I can tell, you managed two things in *your* life: you run away from Hunt's Station . . . then come running back."

Hank said, "We all pissed it away different."

"I ain't pissed nothing away, damn you. Ain't no one plays banjo better'n me. *No one.* I can play that busted-up banjo over there better'n most of 'em can play a whole one."

Lloyd shoved back his chair and knocked it over, staggered into the table, grabbed the broken banjo from next to the stove, machine-gunned a few notes from "Foggy Mountain Breakdown," then slammed the banjo on the table, spilling their beers.

"See," he said. "See. What'd I tell ya? See?"

In Hank's memory . . . it's always late dusk in Hunt's Station, those sepia minutes when the straggling light grains up before dissolving into the coming night. A time when the porch lights blink on and the mosquitoes (there'd still been mosquitoes when he was a kid) fog up and out of the swamps and ponds. When the trees, made brazen by the dark, suddenly grow taller and fiercer, and the frogs chorus. The bats dance and squeal; so do the small children.

It was during such a late twilight that Hank, driven from his father's house, drifted toward his sisters' place. And as he rambled amid that half-light of loss and memory, he too felt himself dissolving into the dark, into Hunt's Station and its night.

He stopped and took a good, long leak, his piss sizzling into the dry earth; he caught the faintest whiff of Dirty Willy in his urine and he shrugged.

Hank stood in front of his sisters' house for a long time, steeping in the shadows that sulked and skulked just beyond the warm, homely light that beckoned through the picture window. Straddling that fault line of past and present, he couldn't go into their house, and yet, he couldn't leave—and he despised himself.

Iris came to the window, squinted into the night, shook her head, and walked away. Slow fiddle music trickled from the house, and Hank thought of boyhood nights . . . his father picking banjo . . . Iris and Alison fiddling . . . him and his mother singing . . . all of them anchored by their love of the music and by their love for each other.

Iris and Alison danced into view, eyes closed and cheeks nesting on each other's shoulders, waltzing their sweet sisters' waltz, even in their dance acknowledging, and celebrating too, that they had only each other to depend on. And when Hank saw them, saw what he had somehow given away without knowing, the tears smoldered in his eyes at what had been lost and what could never be regained.

Glenn Hutchins had been dead a good twenty years, but his shack was still in pretty good shape, better'n Glenn, anyway: roof hadn't give in yet, still had a door, windows weren't busted. Hutch had been the first one in town to throw in with

Sanborn Hunt and his waste management company, and Sanborn'd made him foreman. He'd never had a harsh word for Sanborn, not even when he came down with the blood cancer that killed him and that everyone figured had something to do with that g.d. HWM. So, Hutch was gone, but not his shack.

Hank, who had neither the patience nor the strength to wobble back to town, nudged open the door with his foot, peered inside. In that dry, dusty darkness, all he could make out was an old iron cot. But that was all it took to convince him to step inside; he *was* tired. Leaving the door open, he crept toward the cot, feeling a little spooked about entering someone else's past, and reached to touch the mattress.

"It's dry."

Hank's face flushed and he felt like he was going to throw up, like after your best friend pops you in the arm hard as he can. When he turned to run, he tripped on the warped floorboards and fell.

The voice shut the door, neither hard nor soft, but normal, like Hank'd just come visiting.

"Didn't your mama teach you to shut the door after yourself? You used to have better manners than that."

Hank calmed; the voice was familiar, but he couldn't quite place it. He wondered whether this was how Paul Keegan had died.

"So, how're you and Clare getting on? She happy you back?"

"Sanborn?"

"Ain't Glenn Hutchins."

"You scared the hell out of me."

"Good."

Hank stood and brushed himself off.

"Sit down," said Sanborn Hunt, pointing a ghostly arm toward an overstuffed chair by the window. "Take a load off."

Hank did. Sanborn sat in a chair tucked into the darkest corner of the shack.

"So, little Hank Rodgers finally come home," Sanborn said. "About fucking time."

Sanborn's voice was sandpaper: two parts whiskey, two parts cigars.

"Uh-huh," said Hank, who felt like he was playing checkers with Styles Plectrum; he didn't know what move he was supposed to make.

"Uh-huh?" Sanborn said. "Uh-huh? That ain't exactly the most penetrating analysis I've ever heard. 'Uh-huh' ain't exactly the fucking Socratic method, now is it?"

Hank, in over his head, said nothing.

"All right, all right," Sanborn said. "Let's start over. I'm Sanborn Hunt, remember me? Father of that girl you were screwing back in high school? Good, that's settled. I sent you a note a while back. How come you didn't come see me?"

"Because I didn't want to have anything to do with you," Hank said.

Sanborn coughed—the Hunt's Station cough, the cough he'd created.

"You come back to my town," Sanborn said, "and you start fucking my daughter, and you say you don't want anything to do with me?"

"This ain't your town."

"You're not the only one who ever left and come back, you know. Though most of them do manage to stay away. To be honest, I never expected to see *you* again."

"Life's full of surprises."

"Ain't that the truth. So, tell me, how'd you like working for Puritan Chemical Products?"

"It was a job."

"Wasn't like writing those novels you always said you was going to write."

"Like I said, Puritan Chemical was a job."

"I own quite a bit of Puritan stock. Almost got them to buy HWM once, but they backed out."

"Yeah, I wonder why."

Sanborn laughed, then coughed. He picked up a fiddle from beside his chair and sawed at "Jerusalem Ridge" for some thirty seconds.

"That was good," Hank said.

"Bet your ass it was good."

"I'm surprised."

"Know what I always wanted to do? I always wanted to set that fiddle on fire and play it the way ol' Jerry Lee Lewis played that piano of his. Play that sonuvabitch till my fingers burned up. That's what I wanted."

"We all got our regrets."

"You don't know my mind, son, so don't even try."

They quieted, each man sipping the silence and the darkness as if it were a good whiskey. Hank settled into his chair and edged toward sleep. Sanborn struck a match, lit a cigar.

"If you're going to fall asleep on me, you may as well get into bed," Sanborn said.

"What about you?" Hank asked.

"I know how to let myself out."

11

The Old Home

A dark spring muttering in deep woods . . .

Dirty Willy tugged the beer bottles from his baggy pockets and lined them on the stump; rubbed his bare back against the tree, then slinked to earth, snugged his spine to the tree, and wiggled his wide ass in the dirt like a dog settling for the night. And Willy Menard had known all his life that a living dog is better than a dead lion.

He grabbed a sweating beer bottle from the stump and held it against his gross hump of a gut. Even in that muggy heat, Willy shivered. He opened the bottle with his teeth, rotting stumps grinding on metal, blood seeping at the gum line, beer foaming from the bottle, lathering his hand and arm. He licked himself dry, like some drunken cat, before addressing the WillyBrew at hand. His mouth stopped throbbing after the first couple gulps.

These were his hours, after midnight but before sunrise. He could quote you the quality of dark from hour to hour, from season to season, from grays as faint and delicate as a

newborn kitten to blacks as absolute as a dead crow's eyes. He
could stitch you a quilt of these hours, hours when he'd poisoned
Hunt's Station, when he'd played music to try to balm that pain,
when the townspeople who couldn't sleep numbed themselves
with his beer. Dirty Willy, when he chose to sleep, never had trouble dropping off, though. He knew what he had done, and maybe
why he had done it. He couldn't say whether he was sorry—
he doubted it—but he could say that he'd meant it.

He gnawed open another beer, leaned his head against
the tree, and shut his eyes, but then opened them. Clare Hunt's
voice surprised him that deep in the woods.

He was used to having these woods to himself. And hearing Clare's voice woke him, cleared his head like a dunking in
a cold, snakey brook. He couldn't make out the words, just
her voice, as high and lonesome as the stars. A kind of prayer,
Dirty Willy supposed, almost elemental: lightning riving granite, a blizzard wind tangling the world in gauze. And, in the
end, rapture—her rapture prickling his skin, rippling through
his heart, wriggling into his bones. And he knew that Clare had
stolen his sleep.

Dirty Willy Menard sighed and stood, stuffed the beer
bottles back into his pockets, and walked on in darkness.

The smoke seeming to seethe from both earth and sky, Dirty
Willy paused at Lloyd Rodgers' place before entering Fire Town,
listened to Lloyd pick banjo, maybe the two of them the only
ones awake in all Hunt's Station, though he doubted it.

Willy sat in the road and sopped up Lloyd's playing—
Flatt and Scruggs, Reno and Smiley, the Stanley Brothers, a lot
of Lloyd's own songs—and smiled at the thought that he was
stealing from him. He'd asked Lloyd a long time ago to come

by the radio station so he could record him. But Lloyd'd said no, had said a recording was a prison, that he didn't want to be captured that way.

Willy shrugged—screw Lloyd Rodgers—and when Lloyd stopped playing he shrugged again and stood. There was still Fire Town. Always some new lesson to be learned from Fire Town. Willy figured everybody in Hunt's Station would be the better for an occasional skulk through Fire Town.

A nightcrow crabbed somewhere up ahead, scolding and tired of waiting, and Dirty Willy followed his squawk into Fire Town.

Willy knew Fire Town as well as he knew his own rotting heart. Knew where the fiery pits crackled and cackled . . . where the baked earth turned traitor and would turn on a man . . . the brooks and creeks boiled to sere veins . . . where gushers of flame geysered up through the ground. And he knew, when in doubt, to listen for the nightcrow, his firecrow.

Soon Willy's eyes watered and smarted, his broad, bare back burned with falling cinders, the soles of his shoes smoked. He cleared his throat, hawked, and his spit sizzled. He smiled at the sound.

Then, one, two, three, his beer bottles exploded— "Shit!"—soaking his pants and pebbling and pocking his thighs and ass with specks of brown beer glass. He'd forgotten all about the beer bottles.

"Double shit!"

Beer deprived, Dirty Willy considered turning back. But when he heard the crow caw and coax up ahead, he shrugged and walked on. No use in letting the crow down.

Though Willy felt at home among Fire Town's smoky husks and tinderbox trees and smoldering wrecks, his parents' house, his homeplace, always took him by surprise. The smoke would shift and, as if in a dream—or a nightmare—there it would stand. For a few seconds, he would see it as it had been, white and sturdy, his father splitting wood, his mother hanging the wash, and the nervy chickens under everybody's feet. He still half-expected to see a welcoming light burning in the window, but there was none—never again.

But somehow, the house still stood. Hot to the touch and smudged soot-black, more ember and remembrance than wood, it still hadn't been consumed. Willy shut his eyes and saw his big sister, Jenny, pushing him on the tire swing, saw his mother sitting on the porch and fiddling the baby to sleep. And there was a part of Dirty Willy Menard that was more than willing to stand right there on the doorstep of the homeplace, eyes closed, and be consumed by memory.

But Willy creaked open his dry eyes and saw the near corner of the house glow bright orange. An ash sheered away —the crow scrawked—and floated toward Dirty Willy, who stuck out his black tongue. The ash burned, but Willy felt filled—not like at Joe Bleak's. Those ashes, in the end, had left him empty and hungry.

"For I have eaten ashes like bread," Dirty Willy recited, "and mingled my drink with weeping."

His mother had adored the Psalms.

Again snubbed by sleep, Lloyd Rodgers sat in his chair and stared out the front window. When he saw Dirty Willy shadow up and out of Fire Town, he picked up his banjo and began working on a song he called "The Devil and Dirty Willy."

"To hell with sleep," he muttered.

12

Easy's Getting Harder Every Day

"When I was a little girl, no more'n five or six, me and Poppa were walking down by the old Cheney Mill—you probably don't remember it, got burned up in a lightning strike years ago . . . sometimes, I wonder why this whole damned town hasn't gone to the lightning," Irene Taylor said to Clare Hunt and Maggie Parriss. "Anyway, we were down by the Cheney Mill, and as we crossed over the bridge there, I saw a just-shed snakeskin snagged in the creek. I swear, it was ten foot long."

Mrs. Taylor's knobby, granite hands writhed in her lap as she spoke.

"That snakeskin was caught on a rock," she said, "and it fluttered in that current like some fancy lady's silk stocking. And I wanted it so. It was the first time I could ever remember wanting something that bad. I was never one of those whiny little ones, always begging after things. But, brother, I wanted that snakeskin.

"And Poppa, he says, 'No,' before I can even ask.

" 'But why, Poppa?' I says. 'Why?'

"He didn't answer right off. He lit a cigarette, flicked the wooden match into the creek, took a deep drag on the cigarette, then blew the smoke out. We both leaned over the bridge railing and watched the waterbugs skitter and crash.

" 'Where do you suppose that snake is right now?' Poppa says after a while. 'I know that if I'd just shucked my skin, I wouldn't've gone off too far.'

"I didn't say nothing and he sucked wet on his cigarette."

Maggie and Clare stared at Mrs. Taylor the way she had stared at her father on that bright morning decades before.

"Then, Poppa says, 'You know what my grammy told me once when I was a boy? She told me that if you touch a snakeskin, welcome it into your house, you start craving to go snake. You start a-slithering on the floor and hissing at folks and sucking eggs out the henhouse, and before you know it, you're not fit to live indoors, and if it gets too bad, they'll have to take a hoe to you—or a .22. And if it's the skin from a poison snake, it's even worse, because all that slimy, snaky poison starts creeping and seeping through your veins and then one day you can't take it no more and you bite yourself . . . kill yourself with your own poison.'

"Poppa spits the cigarette butt into the creek.

" 'Did you believe your grammy?' I asks Poppa.

" 'Damn right, I did,' he says.

"And we stared down into that creek some more, that gray, silky snakeskin still wriggling there, teasing hell out of me. We both saw the small fish, probably a perch or a kibbie, gilling close to the surface. And we both heard the heavy splash right after.

"Poppa touches my arm and points at some weeds next the creek, and I see the backend of that snake still boiling into the water, coiling out like fifty foot of thick, black oily rope. We see a shadow in the water and then that little fish is gone.

"It was like it'd never been there."

Mrs. Taylor took a long drink of her WillyBrew and savored her audience's silence. Maggie and Clare looked at her, but they didn't see her. They were still smelling her creek and seeing her snakeskin. For the teller, the tale was done. But for the listeners, it'd only begun.

"Would you mind bringing me another beer, dear," Mrs. Taylor said to Clare. "Thank you very much."

Mrs. Taylor had invited herself to the Hunt place and then brought Maggie, her grand-niece, along. But Clare didn't mind. She never refused good company, and Irene Taylor was always good company.

" 'S funny what you remember and what you don't remember when you get to be my age," Mrs. Taylor said. "Or what you end up valuing most. If Poppa'd let me have that snakeskin back then, I probably would've forgotten about it after a couple days or a couple weeks. But the way he played it—I'm sure he knew that snake was there all along—Poppa gave me that snakeskin forever."

Clare and Maggie nodded.

"I still love the rich, wormy smell the air has after a hard summer's rain," Mrs. Taylor said. "And I'm still moved by the sound of a train whistle keening come middle night. There are things I miss, too. I miss the clink-chink of the horseshoe players at dusk as the fireflies blink and blank. And it makes me sad that the eveningsong of the frogs and the crickets and all the other night creatures has been stolen away from us.

"Sometimes, I think that's why we're so crazy with the music. We're trying to make up for what we've killed, trying to fill silence that shouldn't be. Because silence *is* the enemy in this town. Silence *is* what killed this town."

Clare sighed and Mrs. Taylor looked at her.

"Yes, dear," she said.

"Used to be so easy . . . the singing," Clare said. "But easy's getting harder every day."

And, for a moment, the three women faltered . . . trembled . . . let the silence, that treacherous Hunt's Station silence, insinuate itself into the room, numbing their tongues, smothering their voices. But Mrs. Taylor would have none of it. She hadn't dared the Hunt Place with Maggie just to sit there and shrivel and shrink and quit in the quiet.

"Go on," she whispered to Clare. "Go on."

Clare sighed again, even that small, weary breath an insult to the silence, and rubbed the back of her neck. "It's just," she said, "it's just . . . some days, too many days, when I wake up, I still expect to hear the morning birds . . . and I'll listen . . . and I'll listen . . . and then I'll remember that I'm living in Hunt's Station, that I was born to Hunt's Station, and the marrow-deep sadness percolates in my bones . . . then my room, it starts to seem so big to me, like a town, or maybe a state, and the upstairs a whole country, and the house, well, the house becomes a continent, and I tremble there in bed, overwhelmed . . . and sleep, and some darkness beyond sleep, calls to me; not the good sleep, either, not the restful sleep. But the black sleep of despair and escape, the sleep that feels like sticking your head in an oven or throwing yourself into one of Sanborn Hunt's lagoons."

"My God," Maggie muttered. "My God."

"Sometimes," Clare said, "when I hear that mystery train pining through the funeral-day night"—Mrs. Taylor and

Maggie nodded—"I wish I were on it. I wish it'd pull right up to the roof of this house, all black and shiny and billowing steam, and the conductor would reach down his strong, bony hand and take me away."

"You don't want to do that," Mrs. Taylor said.

"If I didn't sing each day's blues, each day's poisons, I don't know what would become of me," Clare said. "I just don't know."

"We all feel it when we sing," Mrs. Taylor said. "Almost every single one of us. It's a feeling in the pit of your soul. You want to move from your heart into your friends' hearts. If you ain't got that feeling, ain't no use in singing the music. The only clear waters we got left is the music. That ain't been fouled, ain't been turned black."

"When I get up on that roof after midnight," Clare said, "I'm always singing for someone. One night it might just be for Marian and her hard day at the café . . . on another night I'll sing for our men still killing themselves up the shop . . . and on too many nights, on the saddest nights, on the nights when I want to drown the whole town in tears, I sing for all the babies born dead and for those never born, for a town that will never be."

The three women shawled themselves in long afternoon shadows and drank more beer.

"There are no short memories in Hunt's Station," Mrs. Taylor said.

"The music scares me," Maggie said. "It's *so* strong. That night, at the singing. I felt like a candlewick being burned up."

Clare and Mrs. Taylor glanced at each other.

"It's our gift, Maggie," Clare said. "And it can't be tempered. It's burning in our *souls*. It's what we've been given in exchange for living in this hell."

"And if I leave," Maggie asked, "do I lose it?"

"No," Clare said.

"Never," Mrs. Taylor said.

They heard a Hunt Waste Management truck shrug out the woods and weasel onto Main Street.

Mrs. Taylor scowled. "I can't even bear to look at one of those trucks no more," she said. "I see one those trucks and I want to kill the man driving it."

Maggie started to laugh—"I ain't making no joke"—and stopped short.

"After everything, they can't stop," Mrs. Taylor pained. "It's like . . . it's like they're fucking a corpse."

"Auntie!" Maggie said.

Mrs. Taylor looked at her grand-niece and almost smiled. "It's all right, dear," she said. "I know all the words, and I know how to use them."

"Wasn't enough to kill all the lakes and ponds, the brooks and streams," Clare said.

"And it wasn't enough to bank the fires of that devil town," Mrs. Taylor said.

"To drive off all the animals."

"To make their wives and daughters barren."

"No, none of it was enough."

"And it still isn't enough—now they're killing each other."

Maggie asked, "But how did it happen? I've lived here my whole life, and I still don't understand how it happened. What went wrong? How'd we get this way?"

"The men let Clare's father get away with murder," Mrs. Taylor said. "In the beginning, Sanborn Hunt fooled everyone. And after we found out he'd fooled us, the men were too ashamed to admit that they'd been taken by Sanborn Hunt. So they pretended everything was all right. 'Sides, the money *was* good."

"The Hunt's Station men," Clare said. "The wonderful and awful, brave and gutless Hunt's Station men. I'm sick and tired of the goddamned Hunt's Station men."

"Even Hank Rodgers?" Maggie asked.

Clare gathered Maggie in with a look, saw her youth and freshness, saw herself, even . . . and, finally, saw what Hank had sought in her.

"Forget about Hank Rodgers," Clare said. "He's my problem."

"Oh, Clare," Maggie said, "when I saw him that night and listened to him, I couldn't help myself. I'd just finished my song, and I thought I was more than I am. I wanted him, plain and simple. It was like he was the door I had to pass through to leave this town."

"And it was through you he wanted to reenter Hunt's Station," Mrs. Taylor said. "Or the Hunt's Station he'd left behind, anyway. It wasn't you he wanted, Maggie, so much as the past."

"The bed is never fair," Clare said. "Never fair, and it's never simple. I . . ."

Clare rushed to the bathroom.

"She okay?" Maggie asked. "What's going on?"

"Sshh, dear," Mrs. Taylor said. "She's sick."

"Too much beer?"

"Sshh."

After some minutes, Mrs. Taylor rose, knocked on the bathroom door, went in and shut the door behind her. Clare kneeled in front of the toilet. Mrs. Taylor placed her warm, dry hand on Clare's cool, damp forehead, then with her firm and bony hands she kneaded Clare's neck with her no-nonsense grip.

"There, there, dear," she said, working her ancient knuckles deep. "There, there."

That night, after midnight, Mrs. Taylor and Maggie stood with Clare on the widow's walk of the Hunt Place. Mrs. Taylor stepped up, shut her eyes, and started to play her fiddle, sweet and slow—a Hunt's Station lullaby. Neither Clare nor Maggie knew the tune, which seemed to come forth from Mrs. Taylor cold and clear, like a deep-woods spring. And as Clare watched Mrs. Taylor, that old, old woman steeped in the music, still moved by it and suffused with it, she realized that she *was* the music and that that was the best any of them could hope for.

Mrs. Taylor nodded at Clare and Maggie, and the two of them, their hands linked, sang:

I am the last child.
I am the last child . . .

13

Whiskey Before Breakfast

Sleep's scarce in Hunt's Station. The good sleep, anyway. Oh, there's plenty of ceiling staring and night thrashing and pillow punching. And the haunted sleep, where you think a dead uncle who scared hell out of you when you were a kid has just skulked into your bed or copperheads are oozing from the curtain rods or fire stalking the attic. But the deep sleep, where your weary soul drinks its fill, that was gone . . . another dead aquifer.

When sleep abandoned him, Hank Rodgers knew that he'd truly come home.

At three in the morning, Hank sat in the dark and listened to someone flat-pick "Arkansas Traveler" on WHWM. Just sitting, an ache in his chest . . . the coils tightening . . . his outlander skin flensed layer by layer to its Hunt's Station self, so that his wife might not even recognize him. Then again, he barely recognized himself anymore. He was up because of his wife, had started awake and gasped when he thought she'd rustled into the room all lace and lies. After he'd calmed, the sweat drying on his back, sleep snubbed him.

He knew it would be easy to sit there, feeding on the night and the music until sunup. Knew he wouldn't be alone in his loneliness. But Hank wasn't resigned enough yet. He hadn't been back *that* long. Hunt's Station could stain his sleep, but it hadn't seized him.

So Hank shrugged himself out the chair, dressed, and stumped downstairs. He shuddered as he stepped onto the midnight-damp dirt of Main Street, a whisper of autumn in the air that time of night, and brisked his bare arms.

Styles Plectrum grieved alone in Marian's Cafe, playing solitaire checkers—right hand against the left—and conjuring the ghost of Joe Bleak. Hank watched, Styles's hands flicking and flickering as the checkers clacked and rattled against his cousin's absence. Styles playing as if the game were the only thing that stood between him and following Joe Bleak out of town. Styles finished a game—black and his left hand had won—and took a long pull on his cigarette, then an even longer pull on his WillyBrew.

"Hey, Styles," Hank said as he walked in.

Styles hunched his shoulders, gave his back to Hank, and mashed out the cigarette.

"Hello, Styles," Hank tried again.

Styles turned, his face looking like granite that'd been gnawed at by slow but constant water for a thousand years.

"The hell you want?"

Even where he stood, Hank smelled the whiskey on Styles. And though he knew better, knew he should just turn around and walk out the door, Hank said, "I want to report a theft."

Styles stared at Hank like he was seriously thinking of spitting on him.

"Yeah?"

"You know that book that Keegan guy was writing on Hunt's Station?"

"Yeah?"

"Well, someone busted into my room and stole it."

"Yeah. So?"

"So? So maybe it was whoever killed the guy."

Styles snorted. "Big fuckin' deal."

"Styles!"

"What're you looking at? What do you want me to do? Dust for fingerprints? Call in the FBI? Put out an all points bulletin? Give me a fuckin' break."

Styles took another drink of beer; he'd killed the whiskey long before.

"It's like this, see," Styles said. "I don't even know where that Keegan kid's body is. For all I know, Dirty Willy chopped him up and sold him to Marian for burger meat. For all I know, old Sanborn has him stuffed in a drum under his trailer. So I'm not going to get too excited about some missing manu-fucking-script."

"Yeah," Hank said, "be a shame to tear you away from that checker game of yours. Maybe you ever find Dirty Willy, he'll keep you company late at night."

Styles stumbled up from the table, knocking over his beer, scattering checkers.

"You want to go at it right now, cocksucker? Huh? I'll break every fuckin' bone in your body and feed you to the goddamned crows."

His raw, red fists up, Styles wavered in the center of the café, struggling in a current too strong to resist.

"I don't fight drunks," Hank said and walked out the door.

"You don't know nothing!" Styles shouted after him. "You don't know a goddamned fuckin' thing!"

At daybreak, Marian found Styles still standing, his fists still raised, his face more fissured.

Dirty Willy, like some obscene otter, is playing at Lagoon No. 53, what had once been Evans Pond—good hockey pond come winter, but the water didn't freeze no more no matter how cold the weather. Willy spins a steel drum toward the black water then chases it—bare, black feet slapping on black sand—stopping it just short of the lagoon. He rolls the drum, heavier than usual, back up the hill and flicks it toward the water again, chases it and stops it. Out of breath, he leans against the drum and stares at lagoon and sky; hard to tell where one begins and where the other one stops. Moved by the total darkness, Willy grunts the steel drum up over his head and heaves it into the water, where it barely splashes, and watches it sink—this time Paul Keegan won't be floating back to the surface—and then strips and dives into the midnight water, where he makes no splash at all.

"Come in, if you're coming in."

"I come to borrow the stock car," Hank told his father.

"You know where the keys is."

The room smelled of whiskey and smoke.

"You all right?" Hank asked.

"I ain't the one planning to take a race car out to The Whispering Turnpike," Lloyd said.

"I just seen Styles over to Marian's. He's a wreck, gone all to hell."

Lloyd shrugged. "What took him so damn long?"

The father and the son laughed; then the father coughed.

"Look," Hank said, "I'm sorry about the other day. I . . ."

Lloyd held up his hand. "Don't go apologizing," he said. "Don't go telling me that you didn't mean what you said. Course you meant it. And I meant what I said. We had it out. That's all. Men'll do that sometimes. I don't think no less of you, and I hope you don't think no less of me."

Hank nodded.

"I'll bring the car back tomorrow," he said.

"Bring it back in one piece," Lloyd said.

As Hank fired up the '37 Pontiac and roared away, Lloyd sat down with his banjo and roared away with him, picking his "Whispering Turnpike Breakdown," gunning that banjo like a hot car down the backstretch and singing over and over, faster and faster:

There was whiskey and blood on the highway.
There was whiskey and blood on the highway.
Lord, Lord, there was whiskey and blood on the highway.

Hank eased through the night woods, the Pontiac a growling white ghost made furious by its imprisonment. As the car warmed, its heat unlocked the past—those sweet racing smells of grease, gasoline, and rubber. Though Hank had never seen his father race, he'd spent a lot of time at the track when he was growing up; and driving that banjo Pontiac made him feel like a kid again, wandering the pits at The Pines. He smiled. No one at The Pines had ever kept up with the men and boys from Hunt's Station. Not a one. If you wanted to throttle-stomp, they'd blow your doors off. And if you wanted to play rough, they played rougher. It's a wonder they weren't all banned from the track.

When Hank passed Raven's Roost, the crows squawked, and when he got to The Crossroads, still swampy from Styles Plectrum trying to bury Joe Bleak, he almost got stuck. But he managed to nurse the Pontiac through the muck.

For all the stories he'd heard, for all the men and boys he knew who'd died, Hank never considered turning back from The Whispering Turnpike. Even just rumbling through the woods, he could feel the car's power in the pit of his stomach, could sense that the car, like a banjo, could have a will of its own. His father had told him once that stock car racing was just another kind of music, the car an instrument.

"It's as hard and beautiful and demanding as bluegrass music," he'd said. "Only difference is that when a banjo string breaks, you usually don't get killed."

Hank nosed the Pontiac onto The Whispering Turnpike, turning left toward the hill of gravel where the road dead-ended. He forced himself to hold back, let the tires warm on the night-cold asphalt. The white crosses, dozens of them, licked at the corners of his eyes. He nudged the car up to fifty, and it seemed to him that the Pontiac bristled at being reined. When he neared the dead end, Hank backed off. When the men went racing on The Whispering, it wasn't the paved straightaways that were so dangerous as the dirt curves. To do it right, you had to dive off the pavement and slide through the curve, straighten her out, then bomb back onto The Pike for another mile until the other dirt curve that completed the circuit. Of course, at that end, a body could just ignore the curve and razor straight down The Whispering toward God-knows-what. Wasn't a man alive in Hunt's Station who claimed to have followed The Whispering Turnpike to its end.

Anyway, it was at the two dirt curves that the white crosses clustered thickest, mushrooms the morning after a rainstorm.

Hank pushed that '37 Ponny up to seventy, the road still silent . . . waiting, and settled into his seat, his old man's car starting to feel right in his hands. He imagined he could hear his father pick banjo as he drove, the notes coming faster and more furious as the car kicked up. Holding back, he gentled into the curves again, not ready to tempt the turns. But his tires stormed rocks and gravel as he whipped back onto the asphalt.

He heard the two cars before he saw them.

Then, black and spitting fire, they racketed up behind him; couldn't see the drivers. Hank went faster, but one car passed him in a blur on the outside and darted in front of him, and the other sat on his back bumper. As the two cars quickened, Hank did too; but they had him caught in a cradle, rocking faster and faster.

The lead car dived into the curve at the dead end, slid broadside through it, and slingshoted back onto the road. Hank tried to slow, but the car behind bumped him and spun him out, Hank tasting dust and blood and dirt as the other car churned through the turn. But Hank never considered stopping. All that he knew was that he was on The Whispering Turnpike and he was racing. He slammed back onto the road.

The next time, they sandwiched him, one on the outside, one on the inside. First one car nudged him, then the other, Hank fighting the wheel to keep control. He tried outrunning them, but couldn't and they wouldn't let him fall back. As they neared the next turn, Hank tagged the car to his right and dived into the dirt first.

Wasn't quick enough.

The other car tapped him on the rear end and the Pontiac hurtled over the banking and into the puckerbrush. But the car was still running; Hank's old man had built it right.

The two cars ground to a stop in the curve, revving their engines, roaring at him.

Hank popped the Pontiac into reverse, mowed backward through the brush, spun his way up the banking and back onto the road—the two phantom racers gone—and peeled out toward the dead end.

The Pontiac was doing more than a hundred, the engine snarling, tires smoking, the whole car shimmying—and Hank still couldn't keep up with them. He focused on the fire dragoning out their tailpipes as they sprinted into the turn. Hank dived too, a little too fearless, sliding through, straightening out, and getting ready to give chase. But the Pontiac's right front tire hooked a rut and Hank again found himself airborne on The Whispering Turnpike.

The car pitched forward end over end and into the air, Hank's head banging the roof, the back end slamming onto the highway and the car flipping one more time to land on four wheels . . . still running, practically purring.

Hank rubbed his sore head—his ribs were griping too—and leaned out the window and listened, not that he expected to hear anything. He knew they were gone, knew his lesson was over.

Slipping the Pontiac into gear, Hank meant to go home. But there, in that night-deep stillness, the road finally started to whisper to Hank, made him smell the whiskey and smell the blood. Oh, it was a powerful road, The Whispering Turnpike, a road too strong for someone like Hank Rodgers to resist. He brought the Pontiac up to speed—the car still responding after all it had been through—bulled his way through the turns and bulleted toward the dead end.

"Push it, boy!" the road seemed to hiss. "Come on and push!"

The Pontiac shivered up past a hundred, Hank's eyes locked on the looming hill of gravel. But along with the speed, there was rage. A rage Hank couldn't understand, but knew he had to satisfy, even if it meant tackling the hill at a hundred and twenty miles an hour.

"Push it!"

Except for the road's constant, killing whisper, Hank's head was clear and cold-blooded. He knew that hugging the hill would give him the answer to a question he hadn't articulated.

"Go for it!"

Something, some black shape, darted from the woods and Hank smacked it, sent it flying back into the trees. He jumped on the brakes, the Pontiac and The Pike shrieking at him.

Hank shut the engine, the rage draining, and crawled out of the car, his legs cramped and stiff, and hobbled up the road.

"Hey!" Hank hollered. "Hey! Is there anyone there?" A raven called back to him.

He stood there for some minutes by the side of the road, staring into the woods. He knew he had hit something, but—

"Shit," he muttered.

As the sky lightened in the East, Hank walked back to the Pontiac, put it in neutral, pushed it to the side of the road, and then limped home.

He could still smell whiskey . . . he could still smell blood.

Part Three

14

Blood Music

I

Dirty Willy woke soaked in the early morning damp of the deep woods. And the pain, welling from his shattered left hip, overwhelmed him—pain past articulation. He opened his mouth, and the sounds that came out reminded him of a truck that wouldn't start on a sub-zero morning, not even speaking in tongues, really, but more speaking without tongues. He sucked in his breath, gritted his teeth, and tried to narrow the pain, bottleneck it at its source. But this river was too deep, this current too strong for Dirty Willy to deny his baptism. The last thing he remembered, before the pain, was skulking onto The Whispering Turnpike; never saw what hit him; had no idea how he'd managed to get this deep into the woods. The pain spiked through Willy's body; he shuddered, whimpered. In place of his left hip there was only the pain. He tried to touch the pain; his dungarees were wet and sticky there— and that surprised him because the pain itself felt dry and hard and hot. Willy flexed his fingers and moved his arms; he wiggled his toes, though all sensation in his left leg stopped at the shinbone; he bent his right leg. He'd be able to crawl. His hands clawing dirt, he rode another breaker of pain—its pureness shocked him, there was almost a kind of joy in how powerful it was. Dirty Willy caught his breath, rolled onto his right side, trying to drag the dead weight of the left with him, digging his left heel into the ground as a lever. Before he passed out, Dirty Willy craved a hot cup of tea, which he didn't understand since he'd never drunk a cup of tea in his life. Still, he could taste the honey gathered at the bottom of the cup as the darkness claimed him.

Marian wrapped her arm around Styles Plectrum's waist, guided him to her room, and sat him on her bed. She untied his shoes and pulled them off; she tugged at his socks. Styles just sat there, his palms flat on the bed, his feet flat on the floor, as if waiting—or listening. Marian nudged him onto the bed and he went without complaint. She covered him with a blanket, shut the light, and left to open her café; the place'd be mobbed because everyone came out to breakfast the morning of a singing. Styles shut his eyes . . . and waited for Joe Bleak.

Hank dreamed Keegan: like in some grainy black-and-white 1950s monster movie, Keegan looms out of Sanborn Hunt's lagoon, half man and half toxin, oozing and dripping and moaning, his footsteps sizzling in the earth as he shambles toward town. He touches a tree, and it withers. He touches a dog, and it keels over. He touches a house, and it blows apart. The townspeople run, all except Hank, who walks up to Keegan and gives him a WillyBrew. Keegan gratefully guzzles the beer.

Irene Taylor started awake to the sound of fabric being ripped. Panting, her heart racing, she took in the room and determined that nothing was wrong. But, still, the sound had been so vivid, so violent. She sighed, supposed it was time to get up. But Mrs. Taylor, as ever, refused to be rushed. She lay there, staring at the ceiling, and waited for the sleep to drain completely from her body. She still hated waking alone. And though her husband had been dead for nearly twenty years, she had that thought every morning; some things you should never get used to.

After breakfast, Mrs. Taylor sat on her front porch, shut her eyes, and listened. For what, she wasn't sure. But she knew it was a morning for listening, a morning for portents. In some minutes, she heard a lone fiddle sob . . . and sob again. A fiddle sending a warning . . . a fiddle seeking help. Mrs. Taylor went inside, packed a lunch, got her fiddle, and walked toward Jerusalem Ridge . . . toward The Chimneys . . . toward the future.

The banjo, blooded and busted, wouldn't leave Lloyd Rodgers alone. He looked at it again and again, slumped there next the stove, and realized that that banjo finally, after all these years, had possibilities; that, seasoned in blood, it had shed the taint of Sanborn Hunt and the poison money. Lloyd wrapped the banjo's cracked and twisted neck with duct tape and restrung it. Left the bloodstains, though. The bloodstains made all the difference. Picking that banjo without the blood would have been like trying to get religion without the blood. That there was an Old Testament banjo now. Didn't feel nowhere near as good in his hands as his grandfather's banjo—

nothing ever had, not even his wife—but it touched something ancient and dark and bloody within Lloyd and that thought almost made him smile a devil's smile. He took the cobbled-up banjo, coddling it, and settled onto the back steps. But before he could even strike one note, Lloyd Rodgers swore that he saw Paul Keegan capering amid the hungry flames of Fire Town.

"Thanks for coming with me to get the car," Hank said to his father.

"No big deal," Lloyd said.

"Don't know if I could've faced that Pontiac alone today."

"Bitch gave you quite a ride last night, huh?"

"Yeah. Might say that."

Lloyd laughed, then coughed. The two men walked easily, familiarly, through the cool, late-summer woods, the sweat just forming at the small of their backs. Watching them, in their white T-shirts and dungarees, you could tell that they'd once spent a lot of time walking the woods together.

"When it's like this," Hank said, "I don't understand why I ever left Hunt's Station."

Lloyd snorted. "You took off because it's a poison-infested shit-hole, that's why. Don't go getting sappy on me."

"I don't know . . . it's just . . . just that everything's . . . everything's so fucked up."

"Welcome to adulthood, kid."

"I quit my job, quit my wife, come back here . . . just give up. And now everything feels so closed off. Like I could never go back. Like I don't even remember the way. Everything's happened so damn quick."

"Listen, you know I ain't one to give nobody no advice.

Don't believe in it. All I can tell you is that you can do any goddamned thing you want in this world. You just have to be willing to take the consequences. Whether it was right or whether it was wrong, I've always paid for what I've done. And I didn't whine about it, either."

They came out of the woods near the Pontiac and Lloyd laughed. "I always said you was hard on a car, but what the hell did you get into last night?"

Gritted up, dented, scorched, and its back end caved in, the Pontiac waited on The Whispering Turnpike.

"Wouldn't believe me even if I told you," Hank said.

"You'd be surprised at what I believe," said Lloyd, walking up to the stock car. "You know, I really had me a time in this old bastard. Had me a time. I could just stand on it, you know, and never flinch. And all them other cot-suckers knew it. I raced on balls, man. Pure balls. Me and everyone else from Hunt's Station."

Lloyd leaned against the Pontiac, peered inside and shook his head. "Well," he said, "it's yours now. Belongs to you and whatever happened on The Whispering last night. Think you can get it back to town without me? Marian'll let you park out back."

Hank shook his head yes.

"Thank you, Daddy," he said.

His father shrugged. "I'll see you tonight," Lloyd said as he vanished into the woods. "Got things to do."

Alison Rodgers swayed at the kitchen sink and washed the lunch dishes, while Iris, swaying too, dried them and put them away. Alison always washed. Iris always dried. Wasn't something they ever discussed; they just *knew*. Alison was a washer,

Iris was a dryer. It was like when they learned a new song. They always knew within a few seconds who would be lead fiddle and who would back up. It was as if they were actors who knew their lines before reading the script. Alison hummed and Iris hummed—"What Would You Give in Exchange for Your Soul?"—their small music embroidering the early-afternoon stillness. Where their brother had sought release in the wider world, the two women had looked inward. For them, it was more than enough to be working together in a tiny kitchen and humming. They heard the fiddle at the same time—scratchy and squeaky, like some dusty 78 r.p.m. record—coming from the front porch. Alison glanced at Iris, and Iris glanced at Alison, and they almost smiled. Alison shut the water and dried her hands on her dress. Iris folded her dishtowel and draped it over a chair. They found their mother, or at least a shadow that appeared to be their mother, out to the porch, fiddling away on "I'm On My Way Back to the Old Home." She'd come to them before, and Alison and Iris were always grateful for her visits; their mother as a ghost scared them far less than their father as a living, breathing man. They pulled their chairs tight to their mother's, fiddle bows nearly touching, and played. And except for the tears welling in the eyes of the living, you couldn't hardly tell who was spirit and who was blood.

Dirty Willy sat propped against an oak tree, his legs splayed in the road; he'd been crawling for hours, snaking through Hunt's Station. Hank stopped the Pontiac just short of Willy, the stock car grumbling as it idled. Dirty Willy Menard looked up at Hank, scowled, then hawked and spit.

Hank put the car in gear and ran over Dirty Willy's legs.

Maggie Parriss didn't know how to pack. No one in Hunt's Station did. The suitcase, which had belonged to her grandmother, sat empty and open on the bed. Where did you start? How did you begin? What should be taken away? What should be left behind? She felt like she'd been told to learn a new language one day, then told to take the final exam the next. She walked over to the suitcase—it smelled of mildew and garlic—and fingered the fake red satin liner. She remembered Joe Bleak's hand, light on her back, the night she sang . . . remembered her father coughing blood some nights when he came home from the shop . . . the older boys always after her, raging and insistent, wanting her body, yes, just her body, knowing, perhaps, that she was the last, knowing that after Maggie Parriss there would be no more virgins in Hunt's Station. Still, Maggie didn't know how to pack, though she had begun to understand the weight she would have to carry.

Anchored in the darkest corner of the Hutchins place, Sanborn Hunt pleaded, "You know I always loved you, Becky. You know that. So don't do this to me. Don't . . . please."

But what may or may not have been Becky Hunt simply stood silent before Sanborn: her naked body young, strong, and pure, a body arched and ready yet unattainable . . . and Sanborn ravaged by a desire he'd forgotten he ever possessed.

Scraping his gut red and raw, Dirty Willy slithered through Hunt's Station, a virus seeking a host. He wasn't sure yet where he was going, only knew that he had to keep moving, as much as his hip would let him. Willy didn't manage the pain so much as the pain managed him. Sometimes it felt like he had no left hip at all, and other times as if all he had was that hip. In those moments, he sank his fingers into the earth, pressed his forehead to the ground, and waited to sink again into the black river of his pain. He heard footsteps and looked up. Lloyd Rodgers took it all in: the pain engraved on Willy's face, the bloodied hip, the desperation in Willy's eyes. If Willy asked for help, he'd consider helping him, but Willy would never ask for help.

"What're you looking at?" Willy said.

"Pretty rough shape there, Willy," Lloyd said.

They stared at each other—Willy, malignant and angry, Lloyd, benign and almost amused—two outsiders living in an outsiders' town.

"Let me by," Willy said.

"Lot of people looking for you, Willy," Lloyd said.

"Let me by."

"Sometimes you just have to confess your sins, Willy boy."

"Fuck off."

Lloyd sat crosslegged in front of Willy, strummed his banjo and sang:

> Old Will, Old Will can't jump.
> Old Will, just humping up a stump.
> Up come a weasel, bit him on the rump.
> And that's the reason why
> Old Will can't jump.

Clare rested in the womb of her room. Just the thought of walking downstairs had tired her; even the house had become too big. When she had first retreated to this house, had first refused to leave her land, Clare had known what she was

146

doing. She was acting, rather than being acted upon, and that understanding had saved her. But since Hank Rodgers had returned to Hunt's Station, she had lapsed into waiting, into a raw state of expectation. Liquid sluiced from her stoma and into her plastic pouch. And when she went to empty it, Clare saw that the liquid was clear. And when she smelled it, it smelled like the sea. And Clare realized then that her stoma had wept.

Though summer, that aging king, still reigned, November claimed Dirty Willy's virulent soul: crisp arthritic leaves . . . gray razor rain . . . the fields all sere and brown . . . black skeleton trees . . . the pale sun turning her back, with no promise of return. Willy shivered, his teeth chattered; he didn't think he would ever be warm again. He curled into himself, like some wretched caterpillar, and fell asleep dreaming of fire. Styles did at least wait until Willy woke up.

"Nice nap, Willy?" Styles said.

Willy sighed. "Ain't been my fucking day."

Styles started coughing, couldn't stop. Kind of cough that bruises your ribs and tears your eyes. Hands on knees, he finally caught his breath and spit. They both regarded Styles's blood in the dust—dark red, too red. Willy almost smiled.

"Don't say a word," Styles instructed.

Styles's first kick finished off what was left of Willy's hip —"That one's for the Keegan kid"—and his second kick shattered Willy's jaw—"And that one's for Joe Bleak."

On her way to Jerusalem Ridge, the fiddles filling her head, Irene Taylor stepped over an unconscious Dirty Willy Menard, shook her head, and kept walking.

The cold welling from his very bones, Dirty Willy stuffed his pockets with gasoline-soaked rags and blue-tipped wooden matches. And though he could no longer feel his face, no longer feel his legs, he crawled on. And when he got to the first black pond, he snaked to the water's edge, ignited one of his rags, and tossed it onto the water—which, after a few smoky seconds, started to burn.

"Styles! You coming or what?" Lloyd said. "Show's about to start."

Styles, sitting at the very top of the Town Hall steps, looked down at Lloyd and shook his head.

"Come on, Styles. It's the first singing since Joe died. You said you'd announce."

"I know."

Styles pulled hard on his cigarette, almost like he meant to inhale the whole thing. "I can't," he said. "I just fucking can't."

Lloyd nodded. T'hell with explanations.

"Smoke's strong tonight," Styles said. "Real strong."

"Uh-huh," said Lloyd, who'd noticed it too.

"Wonder what it means."

"I got to go, Styles."

"I know."

Dirty Willy stopped at the gates to Hunt Waste Management. He still had plenty of rags, lots of matches. He was still cold. And the pain? He *was* the pain . . . and once he had figured that out, there was no reason not to keep going. On the swampy ground, he wormed his way among the thousands of fifty-five-gallon steel drums, the busted pallets and the black HWM trucks—just another of Sanborn Hunt's toxins loose in the world. When Willy had dragged himself to the lip of the lagoon, the toxic heart that beat at the center of not just Hunt Waste Management but Hunt's Station too, he stopped and listened. The singing had begun—he should be there selling WillyBrew—but not even the bluegrass music, which was the one thing he loved if he loved anything, could warm him. He regarded the lagoon. It belonged to him and Sanborn, as did the dozens of others dangerous and deep in the dark woods. He supposed it served as some sort of monument—to what, he wasn't sure. Dirty Willy Menard couldn't say what had driven him to poison his hometown, but he had to admit that he'd enjoyed doing it. Couldn't deny that. He shivered, stared into the lagoon; still craved that damn cup of tea. As Willy lit the rags that hung from his pants and shirt pockets—finally feeling a little warm—he heard Lloyd Rodgers' banjo ring out as clear as Sunday-morning bells. Willy smiled. Lloyd Rodgers was an A-number-one prick, but he was the best banjo player Willy'd ever heard, and that counted for something. Then, wrapped warm and tight in his yellow cocoon of flame, Dirty Willy Menard pitched himself into Sanborn Hunt's lagoon.

II

Most of the women, answering a different, stronger call, hadn't bothered with the singing, and the men didn't know what to do with themselves. They paced, they smoked, tuned their instruments, and mumbled to each other . . . uneasy raincrows waiting for a storm to blow down out the mountains.

When Lloyd came onstage and sat on Joe Bleak's old

wooden stool, the crowd quieted. They were expecting something from Lloyd. Something more than entertainment. A
yearning they couldn't articulate yet knew that Lloyd and his
music could satisfy. But most of them still couldn't bring themselves to sit: they slouched against trees, leaned on cars, or
stood straight and stiff, as if in review. Lloyd looked down at
the busted-up banjo, pretended to tune it. He always looked
smaller than people remembered, but once he started playing
he took on his true stature. He sighed, looked into the crowd,
plucked a few notes out the air.

"God, I miss Joe Bleak," Lloyd Rodgers said.

A humid wind kicked up in the trees.

"Seen Dirty Willy in the woods today," Lloyd said.
"Crawlin' round like some friggin' snake. Legs all busted up
or something. Suppose I could've brung him into town. Instead
I sung him a song."

The crowd laughed.

"He didn't much like it," said Lloyd, who started playing,
then stopped. "You know, Willy'll probably swear up and
down till the day he dies that he didn't kill Joe Bleak, that he
didn't know Sanborn Hunt meant to ruin down this town. But
sometimes, finally, you have to own up to what you do in this
world."

Lloyd picked out a slow, slow version of "Haunted Road
Blues," each note black and bleak, a rain-spattered signpost
down that lonesome Haunted Road. Each wrenching phrase
an example of how Lloyd Rodgers had always taken the torture
and guilt in his soul and hammered them into art. He was
sweating when he finished. And Hank Rodgers, out in the
crowd, just shook his head, realized you could never know a
man who could play like that—not even if he's your father.

And if he couldn't know his father, how could Hank hope to know anything at all about himself?

"You all know that I ain't one to talk much," Lloyd said. "Probably said more here tonight than I have in the last five years. But sometimes there's things that got to be said, no matter how much we don't want to say them and how much others don't want to hear them.

"Like anyone else . . . I'm guilty for the things I've done. And I'm not asking for no deliverance from blood-guiltiness. But you all need to know . . . *need to know* . . . that I'm the one who killed Paul Keegan . . . that I'm the one caved in his skull, with this banjo."

Then some thirty seconds of perfect silence: like right after a car crash . . . or a man facing the abyss in his sweaty deathbed . . . or a snake in the cradle. For a few moments, anyway, Lloyd Rodgers had made his silence their silence.

The first explosion woke them up. The second explosion made them curse and yell and run. With the third explosion, pillars of flame burst up through Main Street. The first two blasts had come from out toward Hunt Waste Management, but the third had seemed to rumble from the center of town itself.

Certain events never succumb to the past tense. To those caught up in them, they remain as raw and immediate as today . . . *and one night Hunt's Station burned.*

Fed by deep, black underground rivers, flames spire on Main Street, bursting through the road, busting through the buildings . . . Hank Rodgers dives into his father's Pontiac, which starts on the first try. Dodging the flames, he roars up Main Street and sees Maggie Parriss, suitcase in hand, struggling toward the woods. "Get in!" he yells. And after taking one long last look at Main Street—*"Get in!"*—she does . . . Hunt's Stationers scatter into the woods, where lagoons burn like fiery eyes, where roads catch afire and trees come to kindling . . . As the women, fiddles in hand, hurry toward Jerusalem Ridge, toward The Chimneys, they feel the earth feverish beneath their bare feet . . . The crows and the ravens, screaming bloody murder, swarm into the smoke-smeared sky, and soon you can hardly tell which blackness is which . . . The explosions bellow like thunder and the fire rages like hell's wind, but Lloyd Rodgers lies on his back on the stage and laughs and laughs and laughs . . . Clare Hunt waits on the widow's walk and stares down into the town. Every building burns—Marian's Cafe, Bev's Beauty Boutique, Hempel's Grocery—and Main Street itself crackles with flame as the fire licks and creeps toward her house. And Clare says to herself, "I can finally leave." . . . Thick, black smoke, smoke that smells like insecticide and paint and sulphur, marauds the woods, seeking lungs to seize and blacken. Howie Brown, in his number 069 stock car, and Al Crockett, in his number 3, go at it, grinning and wheel-to-wheel on The Whispering Turnpike, where the tar has already started to melt and ooze . . . At the edges of Fire Town an explosion, the earth shifts, and Lloyd Rodgers' house is swallowed by a fiery pit . . . The first fiddles begin, fast and furious, as if the women believe their music can ward off the fire . . . Styles Plectrum waits on the steps of the burning Town Hall, smoking a cigarette, the heat baking his face, and he wonders how Joe Bleak felt at the end . . . Chickie LeClerc's HWM truck stalls at The Crossroads, ravens hooting overhead. Chickie grunts out, raises the hood and takes a leak. As he zips up, a geyser of flame erupts and incinerates his truck. Chickie starts running west, away from Hunt's Station, and doesn't stop until he can't smell smoke anymore . . . Tater Tate, pickup truck packed with as much food and beer as it can hold, plunges into the woods toward Jerusalem Ridge . . . Upon hearing the fiddles, like the voice of her long-dead mother, Clare Hunt fiddles too . . . If you dare stop and press your ear to the baking earth you can hear the poison boil underground . . . Glenn Hutchins' place goes up like a dry bale of hay . . . Sanborn Hunt sits on the steps of his trailer and watches Hunt Waste Management burn—steel drums blow, holding tanks burst, the ground sizzling—his eye drawn continually to the lagoon, which burns fiercest, burns brightest, and he wonders how much poison courses through the veins of his hometown. He coughs, and King Crow settles on his shoulder and lets Sanborn smooth his sooty black feathers.

A scorched and scored stump, Dirty Willy still lived.

He couldn't breathe for the fire in his lungs; he couldn't feel for the fire in his body; and he couldn't see for the fire in his eyes. Yet, he lived, an ember of consciousness trapped in a hunk of burnt meat.

He lay next to the lagoon, cast there by the explosions he'd touched off, and listened to the fiddle music—barely to be heard above the gluttony of the fire—from up on Jerusalem Ridge. He let the music shush him, bind his wounds, press the damp facecloth to his fevered forehead. He was prepared to let the music bear him away. Why hadn't he been satisfied with the music, he wondered. Why had Sanborn Hunt and the poison mattered so? He passed out with the taste of WillyBrew on his tongue.

And as Dirty Willy Menard, brewmaster and murderer,

lay there dying his Hunt's Station death, hundreds, maybe thousands, of crows and ravens—pallbearer silent—descended upon him and lifted him up into the air, above Hunt Waste Management and above the flames, bore him to Raven's Roost and set him before King Crow, who hopped onto his chest and scrawked at him.

And just before he died, just before the ember flickered one last time, Willy knew that the crows and the ravens—his scavenger brothers—had taken care of him, had saved him from the flames.

Sure that Dirty Willy was dead, King Crow plucked out Willy's left eye and swallowed it, then plucked out the right eye and tossed it to his flock as if signaling that there would be a feast at Raven's Roost tonight.

The trees smoldered and the leaves crackled and spit like Fourth of July sparklers, but the road out to The Whispering Turnpike hadn't gone to fire yet. Hank manhandled the Pontiac through the smoking woods, assaulting the straightaways and whipping through the curves. All the while, Maggie held on, sitting in the back on her suitcase.

Crows squawked and scree'd as the car growled past Raven's Roost. When Hank came upon The Crossroads he paused, took in the charred skeleton of Chickie LeClerc's truck—"Screw it"—and slammed ahead anyway, tires spinning and whining but the Pontiac fishtailing on through. Minutes later, he flung the car left onto The Whispering Turnpike toward the dead end—and the road out of Hunt's Station. The tires smoked on the hot tar.

Maggie stared at his back, searching for something to say. This wasn't how she'd imagined leaving Hunt's Station. "I don't understand why you're doing this," she said. "You don't have to."

Hank said nothing, focused on the road. He supposed she didn't see the ghosts—the dozens who'd gone to flames challenging this road—standing at each white death marker, urging him to go faster . . . didn't see the burning husks of Howie Brown's and Al Crockett's stock cars . . . didn't see the wave of fire bearing down on them from behind, The Whispering Turnpike consumed in flames . . . and consuming.

"Talk to me, Hank. Why won't you talk to me?"

He sighed. "I've got a wife and a life out there," Hank said, "and I don't care two cents about them. Even when I was away those fifteen years, I was trapped here in Hunt's Station. Maybe you can do better."

Hank kicked the Pontiac up another notch, the stock car shaking, his knuckles white on the steering wheel.

"Careful, Hank," Maggie said.

"No," Hank said, "you be careful."

He glanced in the rearview, the fire gaining, the ghosts thick as cream.

"There's a part of me," Hank said, "a mean, sonuvabitch part of me, that would like nothing better than to stop this car . . . rip off your schoolgirl's clothes . . . and tear up your schoolgirl's notions one deep, hateful thrust at a time . . . and then do it again . . . and again. But I won't."

Maggie shivered and hugged herself, drew herself back into one small corner of the car.

Hank saw the dead end now, the mountain of gravel, and picked up speed. This was where he was supposed to slow down, stop, give the car to Maggie. But the road whispered, "No!"

The road hissed, "Keep going!"

"Hank?" Maggie said.

The Pontiac shrieked . . . The Whispering Turnpike too.

"Hank!"

He stared straight ahead, jaw muscles bunched. He could already feel the impact rattling in his bones.

"Hank!"

Maggie leaped from the back, leaned into him, and raked her nails down his right cheek; there'd be scars. Hank stomped on the brake, slamming Maggie against the dash, and the car screamed, slewing to a catty-corner halt.

The Whispering Turnpike howled.

"Hank?"

He jumped out the car and started walking.

"Hank!"

He turned. "Just go!" he yelled. "Take it and get the hell out of here!"

"But, Hank."

"Go, goddammit!"

Doing as she was told, Maggie Parriss eased Lloyd Rodgers' 1937 banjo Pontiac up the dirt road toward Miles' Grant —a ghost that hadn't been seen in that town in at least thirty years—with Hank Rodgers' blood and Hank Rodgers' flesh fresh under her fingernails.

Sanborn Hunt watched the fire, fueled by some toxic subterranean wick, advance up the hill toward him and his trailer. He didn't doubt there was no stopping the fire, but he wasn't sure whether he would flee; running away had rarely suited Sanborn Hunt. But when he saw Lloyd Rodgers, his eyebrows afire and his face baked brick red, tramp through the fire with his banjo slung over his back, clothes smoldering, and lugging a five-gallon can of gasoline, Sanborn knew there would be no running away.

"What the hell," Sanborn said.

"You said it," said Lloyd, grinning a grin that hurt his face.

"How'd you get through that fire?"

"Power of positive thinking. How about a beer there, Sanborn? Man can't play if he's thirsty."

Sanborn, shaking his head, went inside and came out carrying two ice-cold WillyBrews.

"Oh, that tastes good, Sanborn," Lloyd said. "Hope you got plenty more where that come from."

The two men sat there silent for some minutes, drinking beer and studying the fire, which continued up the hill.

"Somebody should've done this a long time ago," Lloyd said. "Burn the whole fucking place down."

Sanborn snorted.

"Know what your problem is, Sanborn?" Lloyd said. "You could never admit you was wrong. Even when you was a kid, you'd rather eat a dogshit sandwich than admit it wasn't peanut butter."

Sanborn took a long drink of beer and threw the empty toward the fire. "What I want to know, Lloyd, is why you killed the Keegan kid."

"You want to know why?" Lloyd said. "You want to know why? Because he was going to make us look like assholes in that book of his. He had no right to our story. Our story is *our* story. What did Paul Keegan know about blood music?"

"Another beer, Lloyd?"

"No. Time's wasting. Get your fiddle."

The fire had marched another fifty feet up the hill since Lloyd had arrived. Sanborn came out with his fiddle.

"Ready to get baptized, Brother Hunt?" Lloyd said.

"Ready as I'll ever be," Sanborn said.

Lloyd doused Sanborn with the gasoline and then Sanborn doused him, the sweet gasoline reminding the two men of days and weekends spent working on cars that weren't worth the effort, and the two sat there on the steps and played as hard and fast and fierce as they could, Sanborn on his father's fiddle and Lloyd on the blooded banjo. The men shut their eyes and let the heat from the fire mingle with the heat from their music, and each man—Lloyd's fingers already raw and bloody— would have told you that he played better than he ever had as his skin began to prickle with the heat, as his hair began to smolder, their music of and above the roar of the fire . . . and you almost had to wonder as they sawed and picked who was devouring whom as they played the blood music . . . nothing but blood music.

III

The road simmered, but Hank Rodgers didn't feel the blisters. Thick, sinister smoke coiled from The Crossroads, but Hank's eyes never teared. The trees trembled, but so did his heart. After Maggie had driven away, bearing the future, Hank had been tempted to simply climb the gravel hill that punctuated that end of The Whispering Turnpike, pull up some sand and fall asleep, let Hunt's Station burn without him. But, in the end, he couldn't let his hometown die without helping keep the deathwatch. So, his past in ashes, his present in flames, Hank had dared the smoldering woods—a humid gray forest escaped from someone's fever dream—and finally stood where the woods stopped and Main Street started its descent down into the burning town.

Conscious of—but refusing to look at—the Hunt Place, which stood expectant at his back, Hank sat atop Main Street and stared down the hill, conjuring how the town had looked just hours before. That vision of downtown had sustained him during his years away: on certain nights, after his wife had vanished to bed, Hank would put on Bill Monroe, pour the single-malt Scotch, shut the lights, settle into the rocker, and remember . . . trace the grooves of the past. Escaping into his whisky darkness, Hank'd eat breakfast at Marian's . . . buy a Mr. Frostie root beer and a *Tales to Astonish* comic book at Hempel's . . . hang around Ken Meyer's hardware, smelling the sawdust and tobacco, tasting the steel cool of a brand-new tenpenny nail, listening to the red-knuckled, gravel-voiced men laugh, argue, and swear. The town had already started to curdle back then, but no one had noticed yet—or, anyway, no one had admitted to noticing. But now, the fire covered Marian's the way a fist hides an acorn, and he couldn't even see Hempel's or the hardware for the sea of flames. He shut his eyes and listened, face prickling at the heat, as the fire boiled like crashing waves, as wood spit and cracked like bones splintering, as the guts of a building rumbled, falling in on itself . . . as a dog barked.

Hank looked up, peered into the fire. A black smudge hobbled out of the flames, wobbled a few steps, then collapsed and whimpered as the fire advanced. Hank ran down the hill and scooped up the smudge—On'y, the three-legged dog, who was as hot as a biscuit fresh out the oven. Hank paused before the fire, just two, three feet away, let its heat and ferocity break over him, and was reminded of how his father picked banjo, and he wondered whether that was the size of the fire that seared Lloyd Rodgers' soul.

Hank pivoted hard to run up the hill—toward the inevitability of Clare Hunt—shouted "Goddammit!" . . . then stumbled and fell cradling On'y like a football. Hank's right calf had seized up on him again—no getting away from that Dirty Willy—felt like there was a starving rat in there, gnawing muscle. The fire broiling his backside, Hank gritted his teeth, hitched himself up off the ground, clutched On'y to his chest, and stumped up the hill to Clare's. With each step, he imagined he could hear his calf tear like an old bedsheet. The door was open.

As night thickened, many of the Hunt's Stationers, and almost all the women, had gathered up on Jerusalem Ridge. From up there, the townspeople watched Hunt Waste Management get its fiery due, saw Fire Town spread and grow, and thought that their town might simply succumb to becoming all Devil Town, and shook their heads as Main Street—and their lives—burned. But most important, as the men sulked and skulked in the shadows of the ancient fieldstone chimneys (getting drunk on Tater Tate's WillyBrew), the women, barefoot and fierce, fiddled.

They fiddled to sustain themselves and their men. Fiddled toward the merest hope of redemption and salvation. Fiddled to make themselves whole. And because their music was the one last clean, clear stream of water left in Hunt's Station, they fiddled against the flames.

The fire had ravened its way toward Jerusalem Ridge and now circled it. But the women, bearing only their fiddles and their faith, marched on the fire as one, their shower of notes a counterpoint to the fire's hiss and crackle.

Irene Taylor, no more than a yard away from the fire, stared it down and played as the hem of her dress smoldered. "You'll get no more of me!" she hollered, her knobby joints throbbing. "You'll get no more of us, damn it!"

The women fiddlers' cheekbones shone sharper than ever that night as they beat back the fire, the heat tightening the skin on their faces. And there are some who will tell you that the women did more than stop the fire that night, that some of them became the fire, that some of those angel fiddlers not only stepped over the line into Lonesome Standard Time, where the only clock ticking is the beating of your heart, but stepped over the line and into the fire itself, barefoot and all, and devoured that flame as it had meant to devour them, used it to temper their souls, and sent it howling back from whence it had come.

Hunt's Station was meant to burn, they knew. But Jerusalem Ridge was meant for them.

"I've never, never heard them fiddle like that," Clare said. "It's like they're fiddling against their souls."

Clare and Hank sat on the front steps and watched the fire, which had stalled in its march on Main Street.

"Maybe that fiddling did it," said Clare, On'y curled at her feet.

"You'd think you was the one saved that mutt, way he acts," Hank said.

"Don't matter who does the saving, long's you get saved," Clare said.

A heavy breeze blew out of the North.

"Smells like rain," Hank said.

"Uh-huh," Clare said.

Hank stared at the fire and shook his head. "That fire scares me," he said. "Makes me feel like any second one of us could go up just like that. The poison flows in us too. How much of a spark would it take to touch it off?"

"That's why I sing," Clare said. "To deny the poison, to keep my heart pure."

"It's like I come back here and started turning into a miserable sonuvabitch, into my old man . . . and I liked it."

"There isn't one of us isn't damaged. Not one who isn't afraid to cross the town line. When I imagine our DNA, that magical double helix, I see a rotted, gray ladder left out in the rain and wind and snow too long, its rungs broken or eaten away. And when I imagine our souls, I see X-rays blotched by black spots."

"But I was gone fifteen years, Clare. *I didn't stay.*"

"Sure you did, Hank. Oh, your body left, but you left your heart here, you left your soul. And you finally come back to reclaim them, no matter how atrophied."

"God, I hated it out there. Toward the end, I'd wake every morning with sharp pains shooting through my gut. And then I'd sleepwalk the day, faking it. The only time I could come up for air was with the music. A fiddle would make me cry . . . a banjo would take my breath away. There I was, in New York City, and I had narrowed my world to a dark living room, a glass of whisky, and a bluegrass CD."

Clare laced her fingers through Hank's. "When the world gets to be too much," she said, "you try to shrink it, make it manageable."

"Even Hunt's Station is too big," he said. "But I'd rather

be sitting here next to you in our dead town than back there."

The first fat drops of rain fell from the sky and hissed in the fire. On'y lifted his head, then resettled it on Clare's foot. Hank and Clare raised their faces to the night and let the rain refill their parched souls. A true wind fisted out of the North now, and the rain fell harder, slanting and heavy, as the fire alternately howled and sizzled. Steam began to compete with the smoke. The crows and the ravens chorused in the distance.

"Let's go in," said Clare, tugging at his hand.

"Couple minutes," said Hank, anchoring her beside him.

And when they went inside, wet and tired and somehow free, they collapsed onto Clare's bed and made love as slow and steady as the healing rain . . . as fierce and consuming as the Hunt's Station fire . . . and fell asleep with Hank still quivering inside, Clare still contracting.

Up on Jerusalem Ridge, the women, their work finally done, fell asleep where they had stood their ground . . . the earth their bed . . . the wind and the driving rain their quilt . . . and a fiddle their pillow.

IV

That sorrow train, Clare's mystery train, wept through Hunt's Station, its mournful wail muted in the falling rain.

Clare stirred, shivered, clung to Hank and listened to that slow, melancholy train—blues on the tracks—as it wound through Hunt's Station, hissing and swishing to a halt, then sobbing on to its next stop. Not everybody had made it up to The Chimneys.

Hank woke, and Clare nested on his shoulder. "It's that ghost train," he said.

"Sshh," she said.

They listened to the train grieve through the rain, sorrow through the black-boned woods, mourn the gutted town. They heard the train moan to a stop north of town, toward Hunt Waste Management. They heard laughter, then nothing, save the sizzle of the rain and their own breathing.

They waited five minutes.

They waited ten minutes.

They waited fifteen minutes.

"Wonder what's going on," Hank said.

"Never mind that, Hank Rodgers," said Clare, hugging him as hard as she could.

"But."

"Sshh."

And Clare whispered in Hank's ear, "I'm pregnant."

As she spoke, they both heard the conductor call out, "All aboard!" as the mystery train picked up steam.

"Pregnant?" Hank said.

"Pregnant."

And as they kissed there in the rainy dark, that mystery train, that sorrow train, sobbed right over the Hunt Place . . . right on time, right on Lonesome Standard Time . . . and Clare heard her father fiddling faster and finer than he ever had . . . and Hank heard his father picking banjo like the devil he was.

And all Clare and Hank heard was the blood music . . . nothing but the blood music.